Inked

Memories

A Montgomery Ink Novel

By
Carrie Ann Ryan

Author Highlights

Praise for Carrie Ann Ryan....

"Carrie Ann Ryan knows how to pull your heartstrings and make your pulse pound! Her wonderful Redwood Pack series will draw you in and keep you reading long into the night. I can't wait to see what comes next with the new generation, the Talons. Keep them coming, Carrie Ann!" –Lara Adrian, New York Times bestselling author of CRAVE THE NIGHT

"Carrie Ann Ryan never fails to draw readers in with passion, raw sensuality, and characters that pop off the page. Any book by Carrie Ann is an absolute treat." – New York Times Bestselling Author J. Kenner

"With snarky humor, sizzling love scenes, and brilliant, imaginative worldbuilding, The Dante's Circle series reads as if Carrie Ann Ryan peeked at my personal wish list!" – NYT Bestselling Author, Larissa Ione

"Carrie Ann Ryan writes sexy shifters in a world full of passionate happily-ever-afters." – *New York Times* Bestselling Author Vivian Arend

"Carrie Ann's books are sexy with characters you can't help but love from page one. They are heat and heart blended to perfection." *New York Times* Bestselling Author Jayne Rylon

Carrie Ann Ryan's books are wickedly funny and deliciously hot, with plenty of twists to keep you guessing. They'll keep you up all night!" USA Today Bestselling Author Cari Quinn

Dedication

To the fans of Montgomery Ink .

Acknowledgements

I feel like it was yesterday that I told myself that is was finally time to try to write a contemporary romance. You see, I'd been writing paranormal romances for years but had this idea of a large family who were blue collar and so freaking close. It took words from a good friend and all of my amazing readers to give me the boost to try something new.

And I'm so glad I took that chance with Montgomery Ink.

Montgomery Ink might not be over since Adrienne and the other cousins need their stories, but it's sort of bittersweet to have the final Denver Montgomery find their HEA.

In order to make this book happen, I couldn't do it alone.

Thank you Chelle Olson for not only being my editor, but my friend. I also loved sitting down and going over my idea for this book with you. You make my words sparkle.

Thank you Charity and Tara for being part of Team Carrie Ann and doing everything that I can't do on my own. I couldn't do it without you.

Thank you Dr. Hubby for not only being part of Team Carrie Ann, but being my support. My rock. You're my HEA and I love you so freaking much.

Thank you Kennedy Layne and Stacey Kennedy for talking me down off the ledge each morning with our coffee chats and writing. Speaking of...we should probably be there now because we're on deadline!

And thank you dear readers, for being with me every step of the way.

You are all Team Carrie Ann Ryan.

~Carrie Ann

Inked Memories

The Montgomery Ink series by NYT Bestselling Author Carrie Ann Ryan continues when the final Denver Montgomery sibling refuses to fall for his brother's former flame—the company's new plumber.

Wes Montgomery watched his entire family fall in love, and now finds himself ready to settle down. Except the one person he seems to find chemistry with is not only his twin's ex, she also works for Montgomery Inc. But when the two find themselves in one compromising situation after another, Wes realizes he's having second thoughts about the dynamic woman who's burst her way into his life. Sure she sets off his temper, but she also makes him hot in every other way possible.

Jillian Reid never loved her best friend like everyone thought she should, so she pushed him away so he could have his future. Now, despite fighting it, she finds herself attracted to the one man she shouldn't. When her father's health takes a turn for the worse, and a danger no one saw coming show its face, she's forced to turn to Wes for help. The two of them have fought off their attraction long enough, and each cave to the desire. But this enemies-to-lovers tale might have an ending no one ever dreamed of.

CHAPTER ONE

Wes Montgomery was ready for a cold beer and a willing woman. Okay, maybe just the cold beer since he didn't exactly have a woman to go home to like the other men in his family and inner circle. But he had damn good beer at home.

He rubbed the back of his neck and squinted down at his agenda for the rest of the afternoon. He probably should have written it down in a notebook to carry with him down to the jobsite, but he lived and breathed through his tablet. It connected to his phone, laptop, *and* computer and was constantly backed up in two places. Why would he risk his very detailed organization with something that could blow away on a windy day when they were in the middle of tearing down walls and putting in plumbing?

As soon as he thought about the wind, a hard breeze slid across his skin, and he looked up at the nearly clear-blue sky. Since they were in Denver, the weather could shift at any moment, but for now, there were only a few white and fluffy clouds in the sky, and most of them surrounded the tall and jagged peaks of

1

the Rocky Mountains. He couldn't help but smile at the grand scenery that not only reminded him how small some of his worries were in the grand scheme of things but also told him what direction west was at all times. Seriously, he had no idea how people outside the area ever knew where to drive without a GPS if they didn't have the long line of mountains and foothills telling them where to go.

"So, you're daydreaming in the middle of the day now? Did you put that in your planner?"

Wes lowered his head and flipped off his twin as Storm strolled in. He narrowed his eyes though once he saw that the other man was in work boots and his usual threadbare flannel shirt—as if Storm were planning to work onsite today. Considering that he'd *just* recovered from a near fatal accident, Wes hoped that wasn't the case.

He didn't want to have to beat his brother's ass for stupidity.

The two of them weren't identical, but of the eight Montgomery kids in their immediate family, they looked the most alike, at least according to everyone else. They each had the same shade of chestnut brown hair that the rest of the family had, along with their bright blue eyes. But what made them look the most alike was probably their square jawlines and smiles—though Storm hadn't smiled much before he finally gave in and fell in love.

The two of them were Montgomerys through and through, though. Most of the guys had big beards—though Wes tended to shave his when meeting with clients these days—and all of them had ink. Even his sisters had tons of ink, with Maya having more than almost anyone in the family. But considering she and their eldest brother Austin owned a tattoo shop called Montgomery Ink, that only made sense.

And while Wes and Storm had the ink and even some of the piercings his family tended to lean toward, they didn't work in the family tattoo shop. Instead, they owned and operated Montgomery Inc., a construction company that their parents had started before handing the reins over. Wes ran the books and was pretty much the lead in charge at all times. Storm was their architect and a god at figuring out how to make things work in a renovation or a new build.

Over time, others had come into the company that their parents had created and slaved over. Now that he was in charge, the weight of that responsibility was never lost on Wes.

"What the hell are you doing onsite in what looks to be your gear?" Wes demanded once Storm came closer. He didn't want to yell too loudly in case any of their workers were around. Never good to act like a toddler instead of the boss, as his mother would say. And his father for that matter. "You're supposed to be in bed while Everly and the boys comfort you."

Storm raised a brow. "We're in my fiancée's bookstore, dumbass, of course I'm going to be here."

"And he's not going to lift a thing," Everly said as she made her way to them. Storm's woman mock glared before coming to stand beside them. Her long, ash-blond hair was up in a loose bun on the top of her head with tendrils spiraling down. He knew she'd probably thrown it up like that during her busy morning of dealing with twin toddlers, a puppy, and a grumpy Storm, yet Wes couldn't help but think that Storm was one lucky man.

Not that Wes wanted Everly in that way, but having someone, *anyone* to come home to might be a nice thing once in a while. Jesus, he was starting to sound morose.

"I'm not going to lift anything," Storm repeated. "I promise. I'm just here to oversee and answer questions. These are just my comfy clothes for any work." He slowly wrapped an arm around Everly's shoulders, and she leaned into him, though Wes noted she was careful not to put any weight on him. Storm had hurt his back pretty severely and was lucky to even be walking right then, but he was allowed and encouraged to get exercise and stretch out.

"We'll find you a chair and a station to set up, then," Wes said. "We're not taking any unnecessary chances."

Storm sighed, but the corner of his mouth lifted up into a smile. "No worries. I'm not about to start dancing a jig or lift even a single box. I promised the boys I'd watch them play in the pool that we set up in the backyard this afternoon, and I'm not about to break that vow."

Everly's boys were from her previous marriage, but Storm had been in their lives from day one since he'd been friends with Everly and her late husband. Now, Storm was in the process of adopting the twins *and* marrying Everly.

Wes couldn't believe how quickly things had changed, but hell, in the past few years, *everything* had changed so much he could barely keep up.

His eldest brother, Austin, had married the girl next door, Sierra, and they now had two children— though the eldest was from a previous relationship. Leif was a teenager now, God help them all. Wes's youngest sister, Miranda, was married to their friend Decker, who also happened to work with Storm and Wes at Montgomery Inc. and Decker and Miranda also had a child. How his younger sister had grown up so quickly, he didn't know. One minute, he was putting a princess bandage on her knee; and the next, she was holding her own child in her arms. Meghan, the oldest of the Montgomery girls though still younger than Wes, had married her best friend, Luc, and they were raising their *three* kids. The two of them even worked with Wes every day with Meghan operating the landscaping arm of the company and Luc as their lead electrician.

Their company was a family business through and through, and it seemed it kept growing with each passing month—just like the family itself.

His younger brother, Griffin, had married his personal assistant, though Wes wasn't sure she filled that role any longer and he didn't intend to ask. Autumn always blushed like crazy whenever Wes mentioned it, and he *really* didn't want to know what she and his brother did together once the office door was shut.

Maya, the middle Montgomery girl, had not only married her best friend but *his* ex-boyfriend, as well. Legally, she was only married to one of them, but to everyone close to the family, they knew the truth. Maya, Jake, and Border had had a baby the same time as Meghan and Miranda had theirs, and the three sisters were now raising their kids together. So, like Wes and his siblings, they'd have a huge family to grow up with even though they were cousins and not brothers or sisters. Though for all Wes knew, everyone was gearing up for the next additions to their broods. For a while there, everywhere he turned, someone was turning up pregnant. Thankfully—since he wasn't in a serious relationship and hadn't been since he and Sophia broke up—it wasn't him.

And, finally, there was Alex. Wes rubbed his chest just thinking about his youngest brother. Alex had been through hell and back, and Wes was only now learning the details. But in the end, Alex had come out stronger and was in love with Wes's admin, Tabby. For a while there, most of the family thought that Wes and Tabby would end up together, but Wes couldn't help but cringe at that thought. She was like one of his little sisters, nothing more, and he knew Tabby felt the same way about him. Just because the two of them shared a love of planners and organization didn't mean they were meant for each other. Clearly, she'd been made for his brother. Not him.

And that left him all by himself these days. Alone. Womanless.

And if that wasn't a depressing thought, he didn't know what was.

"You're daydreaming again," Storm said softly. "You okay, Wes? You seem off today."

Wes shook himself out of his thoughts and gave his brother a grin that he actually felt. He might not have a woman in his life, but he wasn't unhappy. He had a job he loved, and a family that cared for him. And for once, everyone seemed healthy. That was saying something, considering they had been in hospital waiting areas far more than any family should, especially recently. They should just name the damn emergency room the Montgomery Wing at this point.

"I'm fine. Just thinking about how big the Montgomerys have gotten." That was the truth, or at least part of it, so he went with it.

"We're doubling each month it seems." Storm wrapped his arm around Everly's shoulder. "But I don't mind."

Everly rolled her eyes. "Considering the boys and I took over your house? I would hope not."

"Well, Randy had already tried taking over, and I think the twins are helping their puppy along with that."

Wes just looked between the couple and shook his head as they bantered. The two of them had been good friends before Everly's husband passed away. Then, for some reason, they'd pushed each other away though they'd stayed in touch for the boys' sake. Now, they were engaged and ready to build their new family as well as rebuild Everly's bookshop.

Wes wanted that, damn it. He'd come close once, and it had gone to shit for many reasons, one being that he'd known Sophia wasn't the one for him. Now, he didn't have any prospects.

He ignored the needling thought in his mind telling him that there *was* a person he was beyond attracted to, but he'd be damned if he gave in to that particular urge.

And as if the gods themselves had called the siren with her own song, *she* walked into the building.

Jillian Reid. Storm's ex friends-with-benefits, and Montgomery Inc.'s current lead plumber.

She strolled in wearing her normal cargo pants and a cotton shirt bearing the Montgomery Inc. logo— the MI iris that was a circle enclosing the letters with a flower on the side. Each of the adult Montgomerys— including those that had married in—had one tattooed on them. It was a rite of passage for their family, and he knew Everly was getting hers soon.

His thoughts went back to the woman walking toward them as Jillian set down her tool kit and stretched her back. The action pressed her breasts right up to the thin cotton of her shirt. He swallowed hard and pulled his gaze up to the blue of her eyes. She worked for him, damn it. He needed to get his act together and not be a freaking lecher.

Of course, it helped to remember that the two of them actively hated each other.

Regardless of how hard he got whenever she was near, he always, *always* fought with her. And he had no idea why they'd started out fighting, only that they kept irritating the hell out of each other.

"Hey, boss," Jillian said with a sigh. She glanced at Wes and raised a brow. "Make that bosses. I checked out the bathroom on the first floor, and it's going to have to be completely gutted. There's no way I can save the pipes or anything there." She gave Everly a small smile. "I'm sorry, hon. I know that sucks, but insurance will cover it for sure. The thing is, with these old buildings in downtown Denver, you'd have had to get them replaced sooner or later anyway."

Everly shrugged before pulling away from Storm to give Jillian a one-armed hug. It would have boggled Wes's mind that the two women could become so close in such a short amount of time, but Everly was a sweet and open woman who cared about those close to her with a fierce intensity.

"Thanks for looking," Everly said with a smile. "And I'd hug you more, but since you just came from digging around toilets..."

Jillian batted her eyelashes. "That's me. Toilets and clogs. It's no wonder the men are chasing after me."

Storm snorted and gently tugged Everly back to his side. "Sounds about right. If they only knew what covered your boots right now."

Wes narrowed his eyes and looked down at the work boots she wore. "What *is* on your boots that you're tracking through my jobsite?" He held back a wince at the harshness of his tone. He never meant to sound like an ass, but Jillian brought out the worst in him.

Storm sighed under his breath, and Everly muttered something he didn't quite catch. Jillian, however, just raised that brow of hers and snorted.

"Don't worry, *Wesley*, I wore booties when I was in there. I wouldn't demean myself by daring to dirty your precious floors."

Out of the corner of his eye, he saw Storm pull Everly away toward the back of the building. His twin was probably getting sick and tired of being the middle of Jillian's and Wes's tiffs. Frankly, Wes was tired of it too, but there was just something about her that got under his skin and made him lash out like a man half his age.

"That's not what I meant, and you know it."

"Whatever." She brushed him off. "I'm just doing my job. Something you pay me to do, right? I need to head over to the Anderson house, by the way, to do the final check on my end of things so you can sign off. Is there anything you need me here for today?" She sounded so professional, but beneath the words, he heard the annoyance in her tone.

"There's some plumbing I'd like her to check, if you know what I mean," one of the guys working on the demo muttered under his breath as he walked by.

Jillian froze for an instant, her face paling before she tightened her jaw and dashes of red covered her cheekbones—from anger or embarrassment, Wes didn't know.

Either way, he was pissed.

Jillian reached out and grabbed his arm as he turned to yell at the guy. "Don't. It's not worth it," she whispered under her breath. "Just let it go."

He narrowed his eyes at her. "This isn't the first time he's said something. Is it?"

She raised her chin. "It doesn't matter. Just let it go," she repeated.

9

"Sorry, no can do." He pulled away from her, annoyed that her touch left a heated trail on his skin. He went to Jeff's side and tapped him on the shoulder. The guy looked surprised for a moment before scowling.

Jeff turned around and frowned before setting down his stuff. The man was around Wes's age but looked far older since he drank and partied hard when he wasn't working. He sneered over at Jillian before seeming to think better of it and turning again to Wes. They were out of earshot of others, but Wes had a feeling if the man started yelling, there was no way to hide it.

"Yeah?"

"First, apologize for that sexist and poor comment. You're opening yourself—and our company—up to sexual harassment lawsuits because you're an asshole. Second, pack your bags and get off our site. You're fired."

"You're fucking kidding me, right? For this bitch? I've been working for this company for years. Hell, your daddy is the one who hired me. You have no right."

Wes's hand tightened on his tablet, and he blew out a breath so he wouldn't hit the man. "I have every right. You *never* treat anyone like you just did. You hear me?"

"Fuck this shit. And fuck you. Must be great having that nice ass to bang when you're not living in your high castle."

He stormed off, and Wes stood there, his chest heaving. There was no way the others hadn't heard that, even though he'd tried to keep the conversation private. But there was no damn way he was going to let that man work for Montgomery Inc. if he treated his coworkers—or hell, *any* woman—like that.

Wes stepped around the corner, and the others got back to work quickly, acting as if they hadn't been listening. Storm and Everly were nowhere to be seen, but he knew they'd hear about it soon.

Jillian, however, stood exactly where she'd been, her arms folded across her chest and her face red.

"Jillian—"

"Thanks for that. I guess. But from now on, I can handle things myself."

He clenched his jaw, anger spilling out with his words. "No. This is *my* company. My *family's* company. No one gets to treat you like that. Or anyone else for that matter. If you have a problem with the way I run things, then you can get the hell out of here, too." He didn't mean the last part, but he was pissed off that anyone would say shit like that to her. And, apparently, this wasn't the first time.

She raised her chin once more, her nostrils flaring. "Whatever, Wesley." And with that, she picked up her things and walked out of the building, leaving him standing there like an idiot.

"My name's not fucking Wesley," he growled, knowing no one was listening to him. Or, at least, that's what he thought.

"Just fucking ask her out already," Decker mumbled as he passed by. "Seriously."

"He's right, you know," Meghan singsonged. Apparently, the two of them hadn't heard what had happened with Jeff yet or they'd be singing another tune.

"Just shut up," Wes snarled and turned on his heel. He had things to do today, and none of them included growling over a woman he didn't want to want.

He didn't know much about what his future would bring, but he did know one thing for sure—Jillian Reid was not for him. Ever.

CHAPTER TWO

Jillian Reid put the last of the dishes into the dishwasher and closed the door. She'd already added soap, so it was just a quick press of a couple of buttons, and her dad would probably have enough dishes for the week. Not that it mattered since she'd be over tomorrow and the day after that to make sure things were clean and he had food. He might be starting to resent her for helping out so much at her childhood home, but that was just something he'd have to deal with because there was no way she'd let her dad not have everything he needed.

Her hands tightened on the counter in front of her, and she let out a slow breath, trying to calm the anxious anger that seemed to be so prevalent in her life these days. Once, she'd been the smiling one, the woman who was sarcastic when she wanted but honestly doing okay in the grand scheme of things. She'd had an on-again, off-again, not-really-a-boyfriend in Storm and she'd liked it. They'd had each other to lean on and were still friends. Only now, they weren't sleeping together whenever they felt like it.

She'd known for too long that they were using each other as a crutch, but it truly hadn't mattered then.

She had more than Storm, of course. She had her softball league and the guys she played pool with down at her favorite bar. She even had her girlfriends that she'd met through Storm since the Montgomerys tended to take people in and never let them go.

Jillian had taken a hard look at her life recently, however, and didn't like who she'd become. She'd used her friends—and Storm in particular—as a crutch, a shield against living her own life and finding peace.

And no matter how many semi-close friends she had or how many times she'd been on and off again with Storm in his bed, she'd been alone. So, when she finally pushed Storm away into Everly's waiting arms, she'd thought she would finally be able to get her life together and find her own happily ever after. Apparently, she was more of a romantic than she thought.

But ever since her dad fell, and everything had shattered around her, she hadn't been able to catch her breath. She'd been so damn scared that she would lose her father, that she'd fallen apart right in front of her co-workers.

Including Wes.

Damn it. If she had fallen apart in front of anyone else but him, she might have let it go, but since her life could never work out the way she planned, *of course* he had been the one to see.

"Jilly-bean?"

She started at the sound of her dad's voice and hurriedly dried off the counter and hung up the dishtowel before heading out of the kitchen and toward the living room. Hopefully, he wouldn't notice the redness of her cheeks or, if he did, would think it was because she'd been working too hard.

"Hey, Dad." She leaned down and kissed his cheek before pulling back and giving him a bright smile.

He narrowed his eyes at her—a trait she'd picked up from him at a young age—and shook his head. "What's wrong, Jilly-bean?"

"Nothing." She turned away and picked up the throw blanket from the couch and moved to tuck it over his lap.

He glared before pulling it away from her, his hands shaking with such severity he ended up dropping the blanket over his legs.

She swallowed hard but did her best not to let her emotions show on her face. Her dad was the only person she had left in the world, and just the sight of him looking so frail made her want to go to her knees and beg God for any kind of promise He could give her. She didn't go to church and, frankly, wasn't even sure what religion she was, but she would start searching if it meant it gave her more time with her father.

More time to breathe. More time to learn. More time to *live*.

But Parkinson's didn't listen to hopes and prayers. At least, not in her case.

"Don't lie to me, young lady." Her father's body might be failing far quicker than either of them could have imagined, but his voice was still just as stern when he wanted it to be. "You better not be worried about me. I'm doing okay for myself."

She gave him a small smile that she knew didn't reach her eyes before sighing and taking a seat on the edge of the coffee table.

"I know you are. I'm just feeling a little blah."

"Man troubles?" He narrowed his eyes at her. "Do I need to go kick some butt? I mean, Storm's a little big, but I can take him. Probably."

Jillian couldn't help but laugh at the thought of her dad and Storm in a bare-knuckle brawl. They'd probably end up rolling their eyes at each other before going for a beer instead.

Her dad just shook his head, a smile playing on his face. "I'm not sure how to take that laugh, Jilly-bean."

"It's not Storm. I promise. He's happy with Everly, and I *like* Everly. Plus, well, I don't love Storm the way that she does, so it's not like I lost out on what was meant to be. We're still friends."

"I'll never understand you young ones these days. Sleeping with each other and not committing."

She snorted. "Okay, Dad, you sound like you're eighty right now, not in your late fifties. And excuse me? I *know* you've been in non-relationships with women over the years. It's not like you've been a monk, mister."

Her dad waved her away, his hand still shaking. "We're *not* talking about that. You're supposed to be an innocent virgin, and I'm the caring dad who gave all to raise you on my own."

Jillian immediately sobered. "You *did* give all. And you did a fantastic job, if I do say so myself."

She'd been three years old when her parents divorced, so she didn't remember her mother that much, though she had vague dreams every now again of put-on sighs and yelling. Her mom had decided that she didn't want to be a mom at all and had left without a look back.

Maybe if her mom had remained single, floating from one thing to another over the years, Jillian wouldn't be so bitter about it, but that wasn't the case.

Instead, her mom had found the love of her life in Boca Raton, married him in a lavish wedding that Jillian hadn't been invited to, and now had two very blond, very preppy teens who loved to play tennis.

Somehow, Jillian had woken up in a bad sitcom where she was the outsider who just wanted a mother's love. It had taken her far too long to realize that she wouldn't be getting anything like that and that her father was the best man in the world. Of course, she'd known the latter all of her life. Yet now that she was looking his mortality in the face, she wasn't sure how she would be able to make it when things took a turn for the worse.

"I'm okay," her dad whispered, pulling her out of her thoughts. "Stop worrying about me. I'm all healed up from falling off that ladder, and the bruising around my chest is long gone. Yes, it exacerbated my symptoms, but I'm going to call it a blessing. Because before the fall, I ignored what was happening with me. I thought it was just a headache or getting older. I didn't realize what was going on."

Until it was too late.

But neither of them said that.

Before she could figure out what to say, her phone chirped on the kitchen island, and she sighed.

"Go answer that. You don't need to hover." He winked as he said it, and she just rolled her eyes. Yes, she was hovering, but who could blame her?

Her phone chirped again, and she heaved herself up from the coffee table and headed to the kitchen. The two text messages on her screen made her eyes cross, and she desperately wanted to ignore them, but since she was the new girl, she couldn't do that. Especially not after the scene that asshole and Wes had made the day before.

Dealing with men and their extremely sexist and dirty jokes about pipes, plumbing, and grabbing long tubes was part of her job. A part she despised and wished weren't the case, but it wasn't going away just because Wes fired one person. Montgomery Inc. was actually the nicest company she'd worked for with many women in each area of construction, but she was the only female plumber. And while it would be nice to believe that everything would be even better now, she knew it wouldn't be. Wes had singled her out, and Jeff's friends who thought Wes—and therefore, *Jillian*—was too sensitive would probably try to make her feel like shit.

She'd have rather stood up for herself without the boss getting in the way.

Her phone chirped a third time, and she growled.

Wes: *Can you come to the bookstore this afternoon? We got ahead on one side of the project and could use your eyes.*

Wes: *This isn't a command, just a request.*

Storm: *What Wes is trying to say as I look over his shoulder is that if you have time, stop by. Thanks.*

Her phone chirped again.

Wes: *Just come.*

Jillian replied back quickly that she'd be there soon so they could stop texting her and stuffed her phone in her back pocket.

"I need to head to the bookstore," she called out as she turned around. She swallowed the emotion clogging her throat as she saw that her father had fallen asleep in his comfy armchair. She went to his side and tucked him in more, then made sure his phone was by his side as well as something to drink and a snack for when he woke up. He'd been sleeping more lately, and she hated that he needed the rest so much.

Pulling herself away from him, she headed out of his house and got into her truck. She was only twenty minutes or so away from downtown Denver where Everly's bookstore, the Montgomery tattoo shop, and a few of her friends' businesses were located. She loved driving around town since the suburbs were all so connected that it wasn't that far—or at least didn't *seem* that far—of a drive most days.

Luckily, she found space to park behind the store since there weren't that many places with the buildings so close together. As soon as she got out of her truck, Everly walked toward her from the back door of the store. Since it was her place, it made sense that the other woman would be there, but for some reason, Jillian hadn't been expecting it. She figured as they moved their way through the project that Everly wouldn't be there every day, but for now, it seemed she wanted to see what she could do.

The place had been damaged pretty badly in the fire that had consumed almost all of Everly's stock, most of her memories of the place, and all of the facade. Thankfully, the bones of the place were still in good shape, and none of the surrounding stores had been damaged thanks to the efforts of the hardworking Denver fire stations. Though the arsonist had tried to take so much from Everly, Jillian's friend wasn't backing down and planned to do her best to rebuild and start fresh.

Something the other woman had done more than once in her life, and Jillian couldn't help but respect that.

"Hey, you, I didn't know you'd be here today," Everly said with a smile.

"I could say the same for you." Jillian hugged the other woman tightly before going to the back of her truck to get her things. "Do you have the boys today?"

She looked around for the towheaded wonders that she had fallen in love with at first sight but she didn't see them.

Everly shook her head. "They're with their grandparents today."

Jillian's eyes widened, but she caught the tension in Everly's shoulders. The twins' grandparents were Everly's former in-laws and weren't exactly the nicest people in the world. In fact, Jillian was pretty sure that, at one point, the couple had threatened to sue for custody or some crap like that.

"Really? Are you okay?" She reached out and gripped the other woman's hand and gave it a squeeze.

Everly blew out a breath. "Yes, I'm fine. This is the second time they've watched the boys without Storm and I there, and it's going well. After the accident and everything coming out about Jackson, they sort of changed." She shrugged. "I don't know that I'll ever feel fully comfortable with them since they were horrible to me for so long, but we're all trying for the twins."

Jillian shook her head before gesturing for them to walk toward the bookstore. "For those boys, I'm pretty sure most of us would do anything, but still, if you need someone to talk to about your in-laws and all the crap they put on you, just let me know." It was weird that she would even be saying anything like that considering that Everly was engaged to Jillian's former best friend with benefits, but she tried not to look too closely at that.

Everly gave her a warm smile. "I'd appreciate that."

Storm waited for them as they walked in, and held out his arm. Everly immediately went to his side, and Jillian had to hold back a sigh. They were seriously perfect for each other, and while she'd hurt just a bit when she walked away from the odd relationship she had with Storm, she was glad she'd done it when she did.

She deserved her own happily ever after, and she'd known for far too long that Storm wasn't it for her. But Storm and Everly? That was pure happiness.

"Hey, Jillian," Storm said with a lift of his chin. "Thanks for coming in today even though you weren't on the schedule. It seems we missed a hidden former half bath on the first floor that the old owners didn't put on the damn plans and then walled up."

Jillian's eyes widened. "You're kidding me." She looked around at the darkened drywall—or at least what was left of it after the fire and the prior day's worth of demo. "How is that even possible?"

Storm shook his head, his jaw tightening. "Don't know, but it sure as hell wasn't on the city plans *or* up to code from what we can tell."

Everly winced. "I remodeled some when I moved in, but honestly, it was mostly cosmetic since the place was a gift shop before I opened. The layout was already pretty perfect for what I wanted and needed. I had no idea there was a toilet and sink hiding behind one of my walls." She shuddered, and honestly, Jillian didn't blame the other woman.

Plumbing was messy, and there wasn't an easier way to say that. There were more days than Jillian could count that she'd had to use one of her *two* pairs of extra clothes she carried with her in her truck at all times because of one mess or another. For some jobs, she'd wear coveralls, but even then...

She held back her own shiver. She was pretty immune to most things she dealt with on a daily basis—backed up toilets, old pipes, and using her blowtorch when needed—but the idea of a secret hidden bathroom closed up with no air ventilation after a five-alarm fire?

Well, it was safe to say she was glad she hadn't eaten anything before coming to the shop.

"Lead the way," Jillian said with a false smile. "Let's see what I get to play in today."

"And with that, I'm going to go call the boys," Everly said on a laugh, and Jillian gave the other woman a real smile this time.

Jillian followed Storm to the other side of the first floor and braced herself. She wasn't squeamish, but considering that no one had any idea this thing had been here for who knew how long, she knew it wouldn't be pretty.

Thankfully, most of the crew was either on another job or taking a break at the moment. She wasn't in the mood to deal with the knowing looks and glares from guys who probably liked Jeff more than her. And, hell, she already knew there were probably whispers going around about her and Wes instead of just her and Storm.

Because why else would a man defend a woman besides the fact that he was fucking her brains out, right? He couldn't just be acting like a boss should and making sure his employees weren't trying to get Montgomery Inc. slapped with a sexual harassment lawsuit. Not that she'd sue someone for that since she knew it would only lead to more issues in the end.

She ground her teeth and pushed those thoughts from her mind so she could focus on the job. It was the same with anywhere she worked. She dealt with assholes who thought it took a penis in order to get the job done. Eventually, they figured out that she knew what she was doing. Of course, she'd never started out with marks against her like she had here since everyone knew she'd once dated Storm, but she'd get over it, and so would everyone else.

Without words, Storm gestured toward a back corner, and Jillian's eyes widened.

Yep, she was *really* glad she hadn't eaten that morning.

Jillian tore off her shirt right beside her truck. Thankfully, she'd thought to put on her normal tank underneath like usual, even though she hadn't planned to work that day. She needed a shower, but the fact that she'd washed her face and hands to the point of reddening her skin and was now pulling on a new shirt would at least take care of most of the damage.

Almost all of the crew was gone for the day since it had taken her much longer to do her job than probably anyone had planned. But, hell, it had been a much larger piece of crap bathroom than even Storm figured. Now, she was ready to go home, drink a beer—*after* her shower—and watch a Harry Potter marathon.

And didn't that just sound like the most interesting life ever.

She sighed and honestly didn't care all too much what others thought of that. She'd had a long day she hadn't planned for, and she just wanted to relax her way.

After tossing her dirty shirt into the garbage bag in her truck since she knew there was no saving that particular piece of clothing, she turned and let out a silent screech. Her foot slammed into the curb, and her ankle twisted slightly. Hands out and braced for an ugly fall, everything seemed to go in slow motion as she tried not to hurt herself any worse than necessary.

Strong arms wrapped around her waist and pulled her up so her back pressed firmly into a *very* hard chest. Her heart raced since she still felt like she was falling even though she wasn't, and she let out a slow breath.

"You okay?"

Of course. *Of course,* it was him. It couldn't be anyone else who witnessed her clumsiness and near accident. It had to be Wes fucking Montgomery.

Where was a crevice in the earth to swallow her up and take her away from this situation when she needed one?

"Jillian?"

"I'm fine," she grumbled. "You can take your hands off me now."

But he didn't.

Instead, he turned her in his hold and looked her right in the eyes. "Are you sure you're okay?"

She swallowed hard. Why hadn't she noticed the brightness of his eyes before? Or the way his pupils dilated when he focused on something...namely her at the moment?

"I'm fine," she repeated. And she was. Her ankle throbbed slightly, but it wasn't even a sprain since she'd had enough of those to tell. She'd just tweaked it a bit in her clod-hopping way of walking.

He didn't let go.

"Seriously, Wes. You need to stop trying to baby me, or whatever the hell you think you're doing all the time. I'm not an idiot. I can handle myself. Why do you—?"

She didn't even know what she was going to ask at that moment because her mind went blank at the first touch of Wes's lips to hers. Her eyes closed of their own volition, and she leaned into him. That seemed to push him harder, and he deepened the kiss, his lips

24

soft yet firm against hers as his tongue traced the seam of her mouth. She opened for him, tangling her tongue with his as she moaned.

The sound seemed to break them both out of whatever the hell they were doing, and they pulled apart as if struck, both left panting, their chests moving quickly up and down.

"No. Not going to happen." She held out her hands, trying to catch her breath. "Nope. No way."

Wes looked at her as if he hadn't seen her before, his eyes a little wide. "It was...it was an accident."

She didn't even flinch at that, too numb from everything else hitting her all at once. "Fine."

She turned on her heel, grateful she hadn't actually hurt her ankle, and jumped into her truck before turning her engine and pulling away.

"Nope," she muttered to herself again. "Not going to happen. I'm not going to do another Montgomery and fuck myself over. And I'm sure as hell not going to do a *boss Montgomery*. Nope. Nope. No. No. No."

And if she kept repeating that to herself, she just might get the damn taste of Wes Montgomery out of her mouth.

CHAPTER THREE

Wes was in deep shit, and he knew it. He was damn lucky Jillian's moan had knocked some sense into both of them the evening before because if it hadn't, they might have done something they both regretted. Hell, he'd never been so careless and idiotic, and that was saying something since he'd had a lot of years to be an idiot.

What if someone had come back to the site for something they'd left behind? He'd have hurt not only Jillian's reputation but also his own for a kiss that shouldn't have happened.

Yes, his employees were allowed to date each other. Hell, so many members of his family were part of Montgomery Inc. it made it silly to put any restrictions about connections on anyone, but that didn't give him the right to practically maul Storm's ex and their employee in the parking lot.

He was going to Hell for sure.

"You're an idiot," he mumbled to himself. He chugged the last of his first cup of coffee while standing in his kitchen in only his boxer briefs and tried to wake himself up. He'd have one or four more later, but he needed this first cup while trying to pry open his eyes before he went and took a shower.

By the time he made it to the jobsite, he'd be bright and perky and probably annoy Storm and Decker to no end, but it was their thing.

He rinsed his cup and put it back under the coffee maker so he just had to press a button once he got out of the shower. He used to try and drink *in* the shower, but that always ended up with watery coffee, a stubbed toe, or a broken mug, so he'd forced himself to wait the ten or so minutes it took him to wash himself. He'd have another cup while shaving.

He frowned and ran a hand over his stubble and thought about his schedule. He wasn't meeting with any prospective clients today, so he'd forgo the shaving. He'd rather keep a longer beard but since Storm, Decker, and Luc—not to mention every other male in his family these days—were keeping theirs, he liked to have a clean-shaven face in case there were any picky clients who couldn't see past a well-groomed beard.

As soon as he got into the shower and let the hot water wash over his muscles, he sighed. He hadn't slept well the night before—thoughts of Jillian keeping him up long past his normal bedtime. He hadn't realized how tight he was until the steam loosened him up some. With a sigh, he lathered up the washcloth and cleaned his body, his eyes still closed since he didn't have a cup of coffee in his hands.

But he knew he'd made a mistake by doing that as soon as his hand trailed down to grip his cock. He jerked off in the shower occasionally since...why not, but now he was holding himself in his hand, squeezing ever so slightly and thinking of Jillian.

He should stop. This was wrong. He was never going to be able to look her in the eye again if he came thinking about her.

But he didn't stop.

And right then...it didn't feel so wrong either.

He let the washcloth fall to his feet, and used the extra soap to run along his length, his breath quickening as he sped up the pace. He rested one hand on the wall and bowed his head, jerking himself as he thought of her on her knees in front of him, taking him into her mouth, controlling him with her touch.

Oh, he might have his hands in her hair, pumping in and out of her mouth, but it was those wide eyes of hers that told the true story. She'd be the one making sure he came down her throat, using her tongue in just the right way to make him come far too hard and fast for either of them.

Then his mind went to her on her back with one hand between her legs and the other on her breasts. He'd done his best to never look at her chest, but he still knew the shape of her. He'd lick and suck at her while palming her tits, pinching at her nipples and humming on her cunt.

She'd come on his face, screaming his name and...

His eyes shot open as he came, hard, his come sliding down the shower wall and his body shaking.

"Well, fuck," he muttered, swallowing hard. He quickly washed his hair then his body once more, trying to calm himself from how hard he'd come just at the thought of her.

Not for the first time that morning, he thought of how well and truly screwed he was. Well and truly screwed.

On his third cup of coffee, this one in his travel mug, he pulled into the new site that sat about forty minutes from his house. Most of his family lived near the northwestern suburbs or nearer to the city, with a few of them living out near Aurora these days, but today, their new job was out near the foothills of Golden. His little sister had actually lived near here at one point, but Miranda had moved in with Decker and was now closer to his parents. In all honesty, though, while Denver might be a huge city out west, driving from one side to the other multiple times a day wasn't unheard of.

Today, they were going to start on a huge rehab and remodel for an older warehouse that had once been storage for a brewery. It would eventually become a small shopping center for the growing community. The owner of the building had already rented out the smaller sections to a bakery, a flower shop, and even an antique dealer that would fit in nicely with the demand of the area. There were two more empty spaces that Wes knew they'd be working on last since the owner hadn't sold those off yet, and it didn't make sense for Wes and the crew to do much more than a basic storefront if they didn't know what it was for.

Either way, this was a damn large job—one of their biggest commercial jobs ever—and Wes couldn't wait to get his hands dirty.

He always found it funny that Storm was the architect of the duo, the one who stayed in the office more than the others since he needed his workspace, yet Storm was also the one who preferred jeans and an old flannel shirt day in and day out.

Wes himself preferred button-down shirts paired with slacks or jeans, yet usually had to strip down to his undershirt while working hard on the site. It was how it had always been, and he didn't question it anymore these days. But, yeah, as twins, he and Storm had their own quirks, and he liked it.

Wes rested his hands on his waist and took in the view. They were in the foothills, so the elevation was slightly higher but not that much considering Denver itself was pretty damn far from sea level. They didn't call it the Mile High City for nothing. The mountains, however, were still far back and they filled Wes's view behind the big building that they were about to work on.

He frowned and took note of the surrounding vegetation, reminding himself that he should look into who owned that land and see if they were taking care of the brush. One spark, and it looked like the whole area would go up in flames. His family had been through enough fires, thank you very much, and it was always a good idea to clear anything that could easily spread a wildfire.

Just recently, less than an hour south near Colorado Springs where some of his cousins lived, there had been three huge fires in a row that took homes, lives, and so much of the land. Some had been because of lightning strikes during fire season, another because of an arsonist who had just wanted to see something burn.

Another truck pulled up, and he turned to see Jillian park next to his vehicle. He'd been the first to arrive since he liked to be onsite early on day one, but he hadn't expected to be alone with Jillian so soon.

He swallowed hard. He didn't plan to talk about the kiss. And he damn sure wasn't going to *ever* mention what he'd done that morning, but he *really* wouldn't bring up the kiss.

So, of course, the first thing to come out of his mouth instead of hello when she walked up was, "I'm not going to talk about the kiss."

He was a fucking idiot.

Jillian raised a brow. "Oh, good. So we're talking about the kiss?" she asked dryly.

"What kiss?" he almost yelled.

Jillian's mouth twitched, and he hated that his eyes went straight to her lips. "You're an idiot."

Yes, yes he was.

"So...new site?"

She shook her head and walked to stand next to him. "Yes, new site." She looked over her shoulder, and he did the same, grateful that they were the only two there. "Okay, so...yesterday? It didn't happen. It was a mistake, and it was probably just adrenaline since we fight so much. And then with the whole almost falling thing... So, we won't talk about it again, and we won't let it affect our work." She met his gaze, and he saw only determination there, something he was grateful for. "It *can't* affect my place here."

He nodded. "It won't." He'd do his damndest to make sure that didn't happen.

"Just make sure it doesn't. It's going to be hard enough to earn the respect of everyone with them knowing I used to date Storm and the whole firing of Jeff thing. We can't add any more drama to the mix."

He narrowed his eyes. "Drama?" There'd better not be any damn drama in his company that made it hard for people to work in peace.

She waved him off. "Nothing I can't handle. It's what comes with the job in my case. It sucks, but it's reality."

"It shouldn't be," he growled out.

She shook her head. "Montgomery Inc. is way better than any other place I've worked. Believe me.

You have a decent amount of women on staff, and management doesn't even blink an eye at the gender of a person when they come up for a job. I mean, you didn't care that I was a woman when you hired me. You cared that I used to be with Storm, but that's a whole other matter."

What he'd actually cared about was that he'd thought she led his twin by the balls all that time, but he'd been wrong about that. He'd been wrong about a lot of things when it came to Jillian. He'd truly thought Storm had pined for her when she was pushing him away, but in fact, the two had clung to each other when they needed someone. At least according to Storm. That had helped Wes's temper toward Jillian recently, but he still didn't want to get into that particular conversation with her at the moment—or ever.

"If there's a problem, though, tell Storm or me. Or Decker. He's going to be in charge of the bookstore while I work on this project since we're doing two large accounts at once. Storm will be floating around the sites as usual, as well. Oh, and Meghan will be in and out so if you need to talk to someone and don't feel comfortable going to a man, talk to her."

"I don't need anyone to handle things for me." She frowned, and he shook his head.

"It's not that I don't think you can handle it. Hell, Jilli, I think you can handle most things, but you shouldn't have to. And this is still my family company. If someone is being a sexist prick, we need to know about it." He met her gaze and made sure she understood. He wasn't sure she would come to any of them so he'd have to keep watch. That's what he did, though, he looked out for his team, and Jillian was part of that now. And now that he thought about it, he'd put Tabby on the task, as well. As their administrative assistant and the brains of the operation—as his father joked—she knew more about what happened onsite than he did sometimes. He still wasn't sure how she did that, but she was damn good at her job and just *knowing* things.

"We good?" he asked after Jillian didn't say anything for a bit.

She let out a breath. "Sure. Now, how about we get started?"

Luc, Meghan's husband and their lead electrician, pulled up right then, and Wes nodded. "Let's."

No matter what, he'd push all thoughts of whatever the hell had happened between them out of his mind. Forever.

They were about done with their first day of demo, and Wes was pretty sure not even a long, hot bath would help his muscles at this point. He clearly wasn't young any longer, and his body was reminding him of that.

The project was so huge, that even with almost all of his crew working on this site rather than the others for this one day, it would take at least four more days of demo to get it even remotely ready for the next step. And that was if he had the whole crew. Since some would need to go back to the bookstore or one of the other jobs they had going on, it would take far longer than a week. Thankfully, Wes had calculated that in, but he still wasn't looking forward to it.

He was just about to go check on the other side of the building when Storm walked up to him. He narrowed his eyes at his twin.

"Why are you still here?" Wes asked, calculating how long Storm had been on his feet and not liking the answer.

Storm held up his hands and snorted. "Okay, master, stop grilling me. I was sitting on my ass most of the day, I promise. And I wasn't here for most of the afternoon since I had a call with a potential client. I'm not about to overdo it and fuck up my back any more than it already is."

Wes went to run his hand over his face, realized he still wore his gloves and thought better of it. Instead, he bent down and grabbed his water bottle, chugging a third of it before speaking.

"Good to hear. And potential client? We're pretty full up, aren't we?"

Storm nodded. "Yeah, and I told them that, but they said they'd wait since they want the best."

Wes couldn't help but smile at that. "Yeah? Cool. But you know, if they don't want to wait, we can send them over to the Gallaghers." One of Maya's husbands, Jake, owned a restoration and construction company with his three brothers, and they were steadily growing. Whenever one of them couldn't fit a client in, they usually sent them to the other if they could.

Storm shook his head. "They said they wanted us and would wait, but I did offer."

Wes nodded. "Sounds good. Send me the notes?"

"Already did. Tabby has everything entered, too. We can go over it later since it's almost quitting time and you look like you need a beer."

"And a shower," Wes added. Of course, just saying the word *shower* brought to mind Jillian, and he had to hold back a curse.

"A shower sounds like a plan," Storm said right as his phone went off. He looked down at the screen and grinned. After nodding at Wes, he answered and walked off. "Hey, Ev. I was just thinking about you."

34

Seriously, every single Montgomery was so in love right then, it was a little scary. Except him, of course. He'd been in love once before, and it hadn't worked out. And though he'd dated off and on since, he hadn't found anyone to get serious with. As the last single Montgomery in Denver, he should probably start looking.

"Wes?" Jillian called out from a floor below.

He frowned and looked down over the railing at her. "Yes?"

"Can you come down for a minute? I think I found something."

Confused, he jogged down the stairs, grateful those were still intact—as well as the service elevator on the other side of the building. Somehow, those two things had been kept up to code even when the place had been vacant for so many years.

"What's up?" he asked as he made his way to her side. They were in the basement that had seen far better days, but Jillian had been working on taking out the old and useless water heaters that would need to be replaced in a different area of the layout.

She knelt beside a large lockbox that looked dented on one side and had such a thick layer of dust, he knew her eyes were probably watering. Hell, he could feel his sinuses clogging already.

"I found this in the wall behind one of the water heaters, I have no idea what it is."

He knelt beside her and frowned. "Weird. It must have been there for ages from the looks of it."

"That's what I'm thinking. It's locked and looks like someone tried to pry it open at some point." She gestured toward the hinges on the side with her gloved hand. "The water heater was blocking the part of the wall where someone had hidden it and probably put up shitty drywall when they did. It crumbled as soon as I went back there, and I didn't even touch anything. Thankfully, it's not a load-bearing wall, you know?"

Wes froze at the thought of how dangerous that could have been and blew out a breath. "Well, shit. I'll get our engineer out here to look at the wall just in case." He had a mechanical engineering degree, but he had another guy on staff these days since Wes knew it wasn't smart to juggle everything on his own when it came to safety.

"What should we do about the box?"

"I guess we take it back to the office. There're a few things for the new owner that we found throughout the day in the back of my truck."

"I don't know, Wes, this seems way older than the amount of time he's owned the place." She bit her lip and focused on the box between them. Wes shrugged.

"I don't know if he bought the whole place, contents included, or if there were provisions for lost and found items or something like that. Either way, though, this looks like something we shouldn't throw away, so we'll store it in the room in the back of the office with the other things. We've done it before."

Jillian nodded and stood up, groaning as she rubbed the small of her back. "I'll help you lift this upstairs because it's damn heavy, and then I'm heading home to rest for as many hours as I can." She grinned up at him though when she said it, and Wes couldn't help but smile back. "I love demo day, though."

"Yeah, it's fun knocking shit down even though it makes me feel like an old man."

Jillian chuckled. "I know what you mean. Ready?"

He nodded, and together, they lifted the heavy box up the stairs and carried it out to his truck. He probably could have done it alone, but since it had been a long day, he was glad he didn't have to. Jillian said goodbye once he closed the tailgate of his truck and leaned against it, rolling his neck so he could stretch out before he went back inside.

As always, he would be first on the site and the last to go home with a new project. This was his family's legacy, and his personal one, as well. He'd put the Montgomery stamp on it and then walk away, ready to start something fresh. It was what he did, what he loved, and throughout it all, he would *not* be thinking about Jillian.

No matter what.

CHAPTER FOUR

"**W**hy on earth did you keep this?" Jillian asked with a laugh. She sat on the floor next to a large cardboard box and shook out her old Little League uniform. "I mean...did you even wash it?" She winced at the smell and couldn't help but melt at her father's deep chuckle.

"Other parents were talking about keeping theirs for memories once the season ended, and since they were doing it, I figured I should, too. Didn't want to miss out."

And that was just one more reason she loved her father more than words could say. It had been the two of them for so long, she knew that he'd done all in his power to make sure she never felt as though it was *just* the two of them. He'd been everything she needed, and he'd proven that over and over again.

"I'm pretty sure they probably washed them first and put them in a sealed bag or something." She paused. "Or, actually, I have no idea. It's cool you kept this, though." She folded the uniform back up and went to look for what else her father had saved over the years. There were birthday cards, photos that hadn't made it into an album, report cards, and even her blanket she'd carried around with her for years. It had helped her sleep when she was sad over her mom, or if she had a bad dream. Her father had worked nights for a long time at his old job and hadn't been able to get the day shift until she was eight or so. It hadn't been too bad since that meant she could see him during the day after school. He'd sleep when she was in class, and then they had the afternoons together. She honestly didn't know how he'd managed to do everything he did when she was younger, but he had, and she was grateful for it.

"You're looking sad over there. What's on your mind?"

"Just thinking about how hard you worked at the factory for me. And you." She shrugged and swallowed the knot in her throat. "I know it wasn't easy, but I never once heard you complain."

Her dad frowned at her. "Why would I complain? I had a job with benefits and a little girl who liked to watch me work and lived life to the fullest. I had everything I needed."

Without another word, Jillian stood up and went to her dad, giving him a big hug. "I love you, Daddy."

"Aw, Jilly-bean, I love you, too." He patted her back with his shaking hand, and she held back tears. Her dad had always been so strong, so solid, and every day, the disease progressed, taking a little bit more from him. It made her want to shout at the sky and ask why. Of all the people in the world, why did it have to happen to the one person she had left in her life, the one person she *knew* deserved only peace and happiness?

She kissed the top of his head, reining in her emotions so he wouldn't see them and get worried, and pulled away. "Let me finish this box, and then I'm heading out to my friend's."

"Storm?" her dad asked, his face carefully blank. She knew her dad liked Storm, but she still didn't know if he was sad that it hadn't worked out, or grateful that at least Storm was moving on.

Jillian smiled and shook her head. "No, Meghan actually."

"So Storm's sister," her dad said dryly.

This time, she rolled her eyes and went back to the box. "Yes, and my friend *and* my coworker." Well, technically, since Meghan had been born a Montgomery, she was her boss. Each Montgomery that worked with the company had a share in it, though Wes and Storm were the main bosses. Meghan was in charge of the landscaping arm, however, and didn't have direct contact with Jillian. It was all a little confusing to her, but they made it work, considering how well the business was doing.

"I'm glad you're going out. You need to do that more."

She snorted and went back to sorting. "Whatever. I go out."

"Having a beer at a bar before going home to relax doesn't really count, young lady."

"As I've said before, you're one to talk. And there might be wine tonight, actually. Since she's teaching me to knit, we figured we'd add wine and make it a night."

Once her dad quit laughing, she glared. "What's wrong with knitting?"

"Nothing, Jilly-bean, but you? Knitting? That's something I'll have to see. You're great with your hands and have patience for pipes, but that's about all."

She'd have flipped him off if he weren't her father. She might be an adult, but he'd still threaten to swat her ass for something like that—not that he'd ever actually done anything like that when she was a kid, but whatever.

"Just for that, I'm finding the ugliest yarn I can find for your scarf."

His eyes brightened, and she couldn't help but smile. "You're making me a scarf? Well, I like that I'm going to be your first project. Maybe I'll wear it for a bit and add it to that box with your uniform."

Her smile was wide this time as she looked up at her dad. "I love you," she repeated, needing to make sure he heard it often and knew it was true. They'd never been good at saying things like that when she was younger, and she'd be damned if she let that continue. Not when...no, she wouldn't think about that. He saw far too much, and she wouldn't put him through that.

By the time her dad went back to his afternoon nap, and Jillian had cleaned up everything they'd messed up during their afternoon, she was feeling a little all over the place when it came to her emotions. Well, actually, she'd been feeling like that for the past few months now, even before her father fell off the ladder and everything changed. She'd been looking for a change in her life, a new purpose, and trying to come to terms with her father's illness hadn't been something she'd ever thought to do.

She was running late, so she quickly stopped by her house, picked up the two bottles of wine she'd gotten earlier for the evening, and changed into something slightly cuter yet still comfortable. While she knew Meghan and Adrienne—Meghan's cousin

and the other knitting trainee for the time being—
wouldn't mind what Jillian wore, she liked wearing
something other than a holey T-shirt and jeans when
she met up with people.

Meghan and Luc lived about ten minutes away
from her if she caught all the green lights. Thankfully,
tonight she had. She'd been told this was Luc's home
before he and Meghan got married, and they were
slowly updating it to accommodate their growing
family. Meghan had two children with her ex-
husband, as well as one with Luc. The two older kids
lived with them permanently since Meghan's ex was
in jail for many things including attempted murder.

She'd sort of known Meghan during her marriage
to Richard, but hadn't gotten to know her well at all
until recently. In fact, when she was with Storm,
Jillian had done her best not to get to know many of
the Montgomerys that well, other than saying hello
here or there. She and Storm had both known their
relationship was better with just each other without a
future paved out for them. Having her integrate
herself into his family when they were only semi-
dating would have only made things more confusing.

But now that Storm and Everly were engaged, and
Jillian was working with the Montgomerys, she was
becoming friends with many of them on her own, not
because of her connection to Storm. As others had
said before, once the Montgomerys drew you in, it was
hard to leave.

Jillian parked in front of Meghan's home behind
Adrienne's vehicle. She hated being the last person
there, but she'd lost track of time. To her, being on
time was actually late, and being early was the only
way to do things. Considering Adrienne lived about an
hour or so away down in Colorado Springs, Jillian
really hated that she was running late for her.

Grabbing the wine and her knitting bag from the back of the cab of the truck, she jumped out and headed up the walkway to the front of the house. She didn't even have to knock before Adrienne had the door open and was gesturing for her to come inside.

"Hey, Jillian. Meghan's in the back with Emma, putting her down for the night." The other woman moved back so Jillian could come in and smiled.

Adrienne looked a lot like Maya, the darkest haired of the three Denver Montgomery women. Adrienne's dark brown hair flowed over her shoulders and back, and she had those swoopy side bangs that Jillian had never been able to pull off. The other woman had half sleeves on both arms, and Jillian knew she had more ink than that. Considering she was a tattoo artist like Maya and Austin, that made sense. She also had a small nose ring, and Jillian was pretty sure she'd seen a tongue ring, as well. All of that with her curves and pinup body? Well, Adrienne Montgomery was damn hot.

And now Jillian was extra grateful she'd put on a flowy top instead of the stained and holey shirt she'd been wearing earlier. It was hard not to feel frumpy around any of the Montgomerys even when they were wearing casual clothes.

"Hey, how are you?" Jillian asked as she hugged the other woman, putting those weird thoughts from her mind. There was no use thinking that at all since none of the women she'd met in this family—married in or blood—would ever purposely make her feel that way.

"Good. Tired, but the usual." Adrienne tattooed hourly and didn't own her own shop like Austin and Maya. Jillian didn't know why Adrienne didn't work with her cousins—or if she had in the past—but figured it wasn't any of her business. All of the

Montgomerys were talented, though, and when Jillian was ready for another tattoo, she knew where to go.

"Same here," Jillian said after a moment and went to set the wine on the counter. "Where are the others?" she asked, taking the bottles out of the bag so she could chill the white she'd brought. The red she left on the counter. She might be a beer drinker, but she knew at least that much.

"Luc took Cliff and Sasha out for dinner and then a movie since they have one more week until school starts."

Jillian grinned and shook her head. "Didn't the summer just start?"

"That's what you'd think," Meghan said as she walked in, a sleepy Emma on her shoulder. The little girl was around eight or nine months now and looked like a little person instead of just a baby.

And that wasn't something she'd ever say to a parent because, geesh.

Emma's skin was a lighter brown than Luc's, and her cheeks so plump that it took everything within Jillian not to go and pinch the chubbiness. She just wanted to gobble that baby all up. Before meeting the Montgomery babies, she'd had no idea she had that ticking clock within her that caused her to act like this.

"What do you mean by that?" Adrienne asked, making cooing noises at Emma. Apparently, no one was immune to the cuteness that was this baby.

"I mean, you'd think summer just started, but if you understood the amount of planning that it takes with two kids out of school, a baby not even one year old, and two adults who are working more than full-time and still like to have alone time? Yeah, summer feels like it drags on and on." She kissed the top of Emma's curls and sighed. "But it's totally worth it."

She swayed back and forth and smiled at Jillian. "Hello, by the way. Emma was having a hard time when I left the room, so I figured since she still has about an hour before she *needs* to be asleep, she can join our girls' night. What do you say?"

"I say welcome, Emma," Jillian said with a grin and reached out to run her finger over Emma's cheeks. She honestly couldn't help herself. And when Emma batted those beautiful, gloriously long eyelashes at her, Jillian fell that much more in love.

"You ready to knit?" Meghan asked. "I can't tell you how much it's helped me relax my mind even when I'm growling at it."

Jillian held up her bag of knitting goods. "I promised my dad a scarf. It seemed better than offering up something like a sock."

Adrienne shuddered. "I looked at a pattern of a sock once. There were like six needles involved or something."

Meghan chuckled, still swaying with Emma in her arms. "Scarves first. Then more scarves. Socks will come *much* later."

"Thank God," Adrienne said with a grin. "Wine, anyone?"

"Yes, please," Jillian and Meghan said at the same time and laughed.

Tonight is going to be a good night, she thought. New friends, wine, and knitting. It was just one piece of her plan to find her peace. Friends came first, then dating. Because she'd told Storm the truth when she pushed him away. She was ready for her happily ever after.

She just needed to start searching.

CHAPTER FIVE

D ays off for Wes were never truly days off, and he knew he should probably do something about that but also knew he wouldn't until he was forced to. He was a workaholic like most of his family. Without his tendency to almost overwork himself, he wasn't sure he'd be where he was today. It took a whole group of people working far too hard to get their company in the place it was, and now that the rest of the family had all married off, it was Wes's turn to keep up the pace.

Today, however, wasn't about work per se, so he could live in his delusions that he might actually have a life outside of Montgomery Inc. With a sigh, he stood up and wiped the sweat from his forehead with his arm as he looked down at the rest of the work he had to do. He'd been neglecting his home office remodel for over a year now with all the new projects the company had taken on. Today, he'd decided that despite the heat, he'd start on the built-ins he'd prepped a while ago.

He could have asked any number of people for help, and they would have freely given up their time for him, but he wanted to do this on his own. At least for today. It was backbreaking work without help, but he didn't mind it. It kept his mind off the list of lists he had waiting for him come Monday at work, the numerous family events he had coming up since everyone seemed to be hitting a milestone or having a celebration of some sort, and of course, *her*.

Wes pinched the bridge of his nose and let out a sigh. He didn't know why he kept thinking about Jillian and that kiss, but he knew he would be better off if he never thought about it again. They'd done a great job over the past couple of days working side by side and not mentioning it. In fact, if he didn't have the distinct memory of him being an idiot and kissing her by the bookstore, he'd have thought he made it all up.

And because of that, he knew he needed to get over it and do something else because Jillian was clearly putting off what happened as a fluke and doing what she had to do at work more than competently because she was a damn adult. He needed to act like one, too.

He rolled his shoulders and glared down at the pile he still needed to take care of before the night was over, but he wasn't sure he had the energy at the moment.

The doorbell rang, saving him from having to lift anything else until after he had some more coffee—or even better, an ice-cold beer.

As soon as he opened the front door, he snorted and shook his head before stepping back and letting his brothers into the room. Somehow, Austin, Griffin, Alex, and Storm had gotten together without him knowing and were now in his living room with toolboxes and coolers in their hands.

"Uh, hey guys," Wes said slowly. "Going out to join the Village People or something?"

Alex rolled his eyes, and Austin let out a groan while Storm just sighed and took a seat. Since Wes had been about to gently nudge his twin to sit and save his back anyway, he was glad that Storm did it on his own.

"There aren't that many construction workers in YMCA," Griffin said dryly before pausing. "Wait, are there? I mean, I only know of the four dudes in the old video, but there are more now, right?" He turned to Austin who, while the eldest of them all, wasn't quite of the YMCA generation.

Austin flipped off Griffin as his answer before setting down his toolbox and running his hand through his big beard. "The only time I ever heard them play was during gym in *elementary* school. And even then they were oldies, so shut it, will you?"

"Okay, old man."

Austin pounced on Griffin, and the two fell to the floor, wrestling like they were kids instead of the grown men they supposedly were.

"You're not that much younger," Wes put in as he sidestepped the duo. "And don't you dare break anything in my house. I'll have to kick your asses if you do."

Griffin looked over Austin's shoulder before pinning the bigger man for a mere second so he could speak. "Like you could," Griffin taunted then let out a groan as Austin elbowed him in the gut before rolling to his feet.

His older brother moved far faster and more agilely than he should for a man his size, but considering he had a teenager and a young toddler at home, he probably had practice.

"Anyway, why are you here?" Wes asked with a laugh.

"We're here to help," Alex said with a shrug. "Tabby mentioned that you put your office on your planner for the day and didn't ask us for help, so we're offering."

Tabby was in love with her planners and organization just like Wes, so it was no wonder she'd made sure Wes was taken care of for the weekend by talking to her fiancé, Alex. "And by offering, you mean coming in and helping even if I don't want it?" he asked, though he truly didn't mind, and from the laughter ringing throughout the room, he knew they understood.

"Of course," Storm said as he leaned back on the couch. "I'll supervise, of course, since Wes will kick my ass if I fuck up my back again."

"We also thought it would be nice if it was just us for the afternoon since we rarely spend time together like this. Decker, Luc, Jake, and Border can be here, though, if you need more help."

Wes liked the idea of the original Montgomery guys hanging out together. They didn't do it often anymore since everyone but Wes had a family at home, and they were all so busy. Plus, the guys who had married Wes's sisters were usually around. And while Wes loved them and thought of them as brothers—hell, he liked some of them more than his brothers on occasion—it was nice to have things like they used to be back in the day. Of course, nothing was like it had been years ago, and Wes was just fine with that, but reminiscing never hurt...too much.

"As long as Griffin doesn't go anywhere near a saw, I'd appreciate the help." Wes smiled as Griffin stood up and wiped off his jeans—as if Wes would dare have dirt and crap on his floor. It's like he didn't even know him.

"It was one time," Griffin complained yet again. "And no one died or lost a limb."

Storm snorted and stood up with Alex's help. Wes didn't think Storm actually needed the aid in standing, but it probably made Alex feel better, and Everly would probably hear about it and be relieved, as well.

"If you have to clarify any accident with a saw like that, then there's no way we're ever letting you touch one again," Wes put in and ducked out of the way as Griffin came at him.

"And no roughhousing next to the construction equipment," Austin put in. "Don't make me call Dad." He paused. "Or Mom."

The rest of them laughed and went back to Wes's office. The idea of tattling on them to their mother made Wes grin. It had been a while since he'd just relaxed—even while doing heavy lifting—with his brothers, and he knew as time went on, days like this would become fewer and farther between. Not all families were as close at the Montgomerys, and he knew he had to be grateful that they even saw each other as much as they did. But for now, he'd take what he could get and relish it.

The Montgomerys could soothe a soul and patch up any wanting he could feel, and for that, he knew he'd never take them for granted. Ever.

It was still light out when the guys left, but just barely. They all had to get home to their families for dinner, leaving Wes alone to scrounge up something for himself. Each brother had offered for him to come over and eat with them and their families, and he knew they'd been talking to the girls during the day since Maya, Miranda, *and* Meghan had texted the same, but he'd sent everyone on their ways. He didn't need a pity invite, even if the others might not have felt it was one. Just because he was the last single Montgomery didn't mean he was lonely.

Well, at least not all the time.

Now that the guys were gone and his office was mostly complete, he was alone in his house, sweaty, and oddly starving. They'd snacked a bit on what Alex had brought them in his cooler, but now he was ready for real food. His stomach growled as if it agreed with his assessment. He stripped off his shirt to wipe off most of the sweat and dust and then went back to his bedroom to toss it in the hamper. He figured he'd shower after he ate since he was a little too hungry to think about anything else at the moment.

He was just about to head to the kitchen when his doorbell rang again. Thinking one of his brothers had forgotten something or were back to drag him to dinner, he opened the door without looking.

And froze.

He'd gone back in time. That had to be it. There was no other possible explanation for why *she* would be on his doorstep.

"Sophia," he whispered.

His ex-fiancée.

The woman he hadn't seen in *years*—and with good reason.

Well, he'd asked the Universe for help getting his mind off work and Jillian, and now it seemed he would regret that favor.

"Hi, Wes," the possible figment of his imagination said. She stood with her shoulders straight, but not too far back as to look overconfident. Her long, dark hair lay in waves over her shoulders while bangs framed her face. Her bright, caramel-colored eyes bored into him, and he tried to come up with what he could say while he took in the rest of her.

She'd filled out since he last saw her, and he thought it suited her. A ruby-red dress fell to her knees in a slight flair while the rest of the fabric clung to her curves. She had a sweetheart neckline that only emphasized her chest, though he was pretty sure that part of her hadn't changed since he saw her last. She wore no jewelry except for a thin silver bracelet around her wrist, and her makeup was perfectly done. Her lips matched her dress, ruby-colored and sparkling under the fading sun in the sky and his porch light.

"What are you doing here?" he asked, not unkindly. He'd never hated Sophia, but she hadn't been good for him.

"Can I come in?" she asked, her voice hesitant, yet stronger than he remembered from back when they'd been together. "I won't stay past my welcome, but I'd like to talk."

He swallowed hard and took a step back without thinking. She brushed past him, and he thought the graze of her curves to his front was deliberate, but he'd never been sure about Sophia.

Wes cleared his throat, deciding to see what she wanted and get out of his head. This might be out of the blue, but he didn't have to be a complete asshole about what the heck was going on...at least not yet.

"Your place looks different," she said softly, her back to him.

He stuffed his hands into his pockets, aware he wasn't wearing a shirt at the moment and was covered in sweat and dust and not looking his best. But hell, it wasn't as if he'd been expecting his ex to show up out of the blue.

"I've remodeled some," he said softly. "You look...good."

She turned to face him fully and smiled, her eyes brightening. "Thank you. I *feel* good." Her gaze traveled over his body, and he held back a sigh. He really should have put on a shirt. "You look good, too."

"If you'll give me one moment." He gestured toward the dining table instead of the couch so she wouldn't get too comfortable and stay too long since he had no idea why she was here in the first place. "Take a seat."

He practically ran back to his bedroom, threw on a cotton shirt from his chest of drawers, and was back in the front of the house in less than a minute. While she might have seen and touched every inch of him back in the day, he needed a little more armor to deal with Sophia and what she could possibly need at the moment.

"So, what are you doing here, Sophia?" He was aware that this was the second time in as many minutes that he'd asked that question, and she hadn't responded the first time.

She stood up from where she was sitting at his large, oak table and gave a delicate shrug. "I wanted to see you."

Annoyed, he snorted. "You saw me, Sophia. You didn't have to come to my house out of nowhere to do that, so why don't you explain why you're really here."

She looked up at him with her big eyes and long lashes and sighed. "Was it really all that bad?"

He held back the curse he wanted to say and thought *yes, it really was all that bad.* Sure, there had been good times, but those were few and far between—especially at the end of their relationship.

He'd thought he loved her and planned to marry her, but she hadn't felt the same way. Sophia had been a thrill seeker, an adrenaline junkie that had nothing to do with extreme sports.

She gambled and used her credit—and sometimes his—for high-end shopping she couldn't afford. She got into so much debt, he'd had to save her—twice—from going bankrupt or doing something worse like credit card fraud.

Sophia hadn't always been that way, or maybe she had, and he'd been too blind to see it. She'd been sweet and had similar interests as he did—at least in the beginning. When he realized she had a problem, it had been too late. She drank too much when she gambled, but she never drank at home. He knew she'd tried a few recreational drugs, but he hadn't found out about that until she left him.

And yet after everything she'd done to him and his trust, she'd been the one to leave him for another man. Wes hadn't been able to stop trying to help her and had screwed himself over instead. That was why he'd never told his family why he and Sophia broke off the engagement. They had their guesses, of course, but no one really mentioned her because she hadn't been a part of their lives as much as the other significant others threaded throughout the Montgomerys.

That probably should have told him something, but he'd needed perspective to understand that.

"I'm sorry," she said softly, breaking through his thoughts. "I'm sorry I was an idiot and an addict. I'm *still* an addict, but I'm in recovery." She rolled her shoulders back as if gaining strength. "You deserved so much better than a liar and a cheat. You *still* do. It took me hitting rock bottom more than once for me to realize that I gambled away the best part of my life because I was so stupid."

He listened to her but didn't really know what he was going to say. His brother, Alex, was an addict and had gone through his own steps of recovery. Wes had listened and opened his arms to his baby brother because he'd known the strength of the man beneath the bruises of bad decisions and addiction.

Wes wasn't sure he'd ever truly known Sophia.

"I'm here to not only say I'm sorry but to pay you back." She pulled out an envelope from her purse and held it out to him. "It's a cashier's check, so it's not going to bounce. And I didn't want to carry cash around with me like that."

He frowned at her but took the envelope, aware that forcing her to hold it would just make him an ass. "You didn't need to pay me back."

"Yes, I did. There are no excuses I can make for what I did in the past other than to say I am sorry and that I'm not that woman anymore. I have my life together." She let out a breath. "I missed you."

His jaw tensed. "Sophia."

"I did. I missed what we could have had together. Not what we had because I ruined that, but I missed what could have been."

His head ached, and his stomach no longer growled—she'd taken away his appetite once his mind dug up all of those old memories. He had no idea what he was going to say and, thankfully, his phone rang in his pocket before he had to come up with something.

"One second," he said to Sophia, who nodded patiently. "Yes?"

He hadn't bothered to look at the screen before he answered, so he had to hold in his shock at the sound of Jillian's voice on the other end of the call.

"Hey. I know it's Saturday night, and I shouldn't be working, but I needed busy work," she began as way of hello. "Anyway, I can't find that one form we talked about yesterday morning. Is it printed out in the office? Or in one of these folders? Or can I print one out at home?" she continued, and he nodded along as if she could see him.

"It's in the shared folder under deadlines," he answered. "If you can't find it, don't worry about it. It's Saturday, Jillian." He couldn't help but smile at the fact that she was doing what he probably would have been doing if he hadn't had unexpected company.

"Oh, I know, believe me."

"Wes, darling? Are you coming back to finish what we started."

Wes could have cursed. Instead, he looked over his shoulder and glared at Sophia. What the fuck was going on?

Jillian was so quiet for a moment, he was afraid she'd hung up.

"Jilli?"

"Oh...uh...I guess you're busy. I'll let you go." She disconnected the call before he could tell her what was going on—not that he actually *knew* what was going on. He stuffed his phone back into his pocket so he could glare at Sophia.

"Okay, Sophia. I don't know what that was, but you wanted to talk? Let's talk."

He hoped he wasn't making a mistake by letting her have her say because, honestly, he had no idea what he was doing. Jillian wasn't his, and they had nothing going on except for a kiss that they'd both denied ever happened.

Sophia, on the other hand, was a woman he had a history with. If she were here for her recovery like she said, he owed it to their past to hear her out.

And even as he thought that, he knew he was once again probably making a mistake, but he couldn't help himself. Mistakes were clearly his forte these days. As always.

CHAPTER SIX

Jillian had spent a week working so hard on the warehouse project that she hadn't been able to focus on anything else but her job and her aching muscles. That was the only way she'd been able to keep going after making yet another fool of herself by calling Wes last weekend. Yes, she'd actually needed help with work, but the aching twinge that had occurred when she heard the other woman's voice just annoyed her.

Wes Montgomery wasn't *hers*. None of the Montgomerys were, and that was how she liked it.

In fact, she had a date *tonight* with a nice man. A *second* date—something she hadn't had in far too long. So those annoying feelings she'd had in a moment of weakness for a certain Montgomery could go take a flying leap off the top of the warehouse.

Clark was sweet, if a little *too* sweet, and seemed like a wonderful man. She'd told Storm the truth: that she wanted to find her own happily ever after. Going out with men on dates was part of that plan. So far, she'd been on four different first dates, but none of them had stuck. The first ones were a little too...boring for her, and there hadn't been a lick of chemistry. Clark at least had a small spark that could maybe one day turn into the inferno she felt with—

Nope. Not thinking about him.

Ever.

"You doing okay over here?" Storm asked as he walked up to her.

She nodded and put the rest of her equipment away, knowing it was the end of the workday and the week. The Montgomerys gave their workers weekends off most projects, and for that, many of the crew were grateful. Jillian just liked it because that meant she got to spend more time with her dad.

"Yep, almost done cleaning up. How about you? Were you sitting on your throne most of the day?" She smiled at that, and Storm gave her the finger.

She and Everly had gone out and bought a camping chair that was surprisingly comfortable, good for Storm's back, and easy to get in and out of— something that rarely happened in chairs that could be folded up quickly. It had also come with a folding table that had a nice cup holder and a place for a lamp, and now Storm had his portable office that no one would dare mess with him about. Well, no one other than Jillian and Wes's family. The rest of the crew wouldn't dare snicker because they'd heard about how badly Storm had been hurt and knew he was lucky to be alive, let alone walking.

As for Jillian, well, if she didn't joke about it, then the bile that constantly coated her tongue would make another appearance, and she'd sob right into the man's flannel.

"My throne was quite comfy, and Wes even took a photo of me sitting in it to send to Everly." He shook his head, a smile playing on his lips. "You guys worry about me too much."

She narrowed her eyes. "No, we don't, actually. We worry about you just enough, and maybe *not* enough in some cases."

"If that's how you feel," he hedged. "But, Jillian? I'm not going to fuck up my recovery. I have two boys, a dog, and a woman I love waiting for me to be able to dance and play with them without wincing. I'm not going to lose that because I'm trying to act macho in front of the guys or something."

If he'd been any other man, the idea that he could so freely profess his love for another woman in front of her might have hurt, but this was *Storm*. She could never be jealous of what he and Everly shared. Sure, she could be jealous that she didn't have it, but never of the fact that she didn't have Storm himself. The two of them had never loved each other the right way, and the fact that they could be close now proved that. He was one of her best friends, maybe her *best* friend, and she wouldn't allow anything to jeopardize that.

Including getting hung up on his twin.

"I trust you, but I'll still mother hen you. It's in my nature."

Storm nodded, his gaze on hers. "How's your dad?" he asked softly.

She swallowed hard. "Pretty much the same since you asked the last time. Thanks for coming over and watching the game with him, by the way. He really enjoyed it even if he probably didn't say so."

Storm smiled. "He said so, actually. Next time, he wants me to bring the boys. Everly's fine with it if you are."

She couldn't help but grin. "Yeah? If you think James and Nathan would enjoy themselves, go for it.

He always loved kids, and I think he kind of wishes he'd had more than just me, you know?"

Storm squeezed her shoulder before taking a step back. They were always careful about how they acted around one another on the job site. It was one thing to remain as close friends as they were with people who understood them, it was another to do so where it could hurt her reputation even more on the jobsite.

"Your dad had enough on his plate with you, I'd say."

She rolled her eyes and bent over to finish cleaning up. "Go home to your babies, Storm. I'm almost done here."

He frowned and looked around at the emptying building. "I don't want to leave you alone."

Men.

"I'm not alone, and probably won't be the last one here. I'm safe enough with the security you have going on at the gate." It was a precaution they had at each site after-hours and sometimes during the day, as well. It was just plain smart with so many dangerous and expensive materials going in and out every day.

"I've become a mother hen just like you."

"Become?" She shook her head with a laugh. "Storm, honey, you've *always* been a mother hen. Now go before I text Everly that you lifted something you shouldn't have."

He held up his hands in mock surrender and walked out of the room backwards, his eyes dancing with laughter.

Jillian lifted her large case and headed back to the open main floor area to make sure she'd picked up all her things. With the scope of this project, she had the potential to run herself ragged if she weren't careful. Thankfully, the company planned to hire another plumber to work with her so she'd be able to delegate.

An odd sound came from the back corner, and she frowned. And though the light was fading and she knew if she weren't careful she'd end up in a horror movie of her own, she set her bag down and made her way toward the sound. There were still some people working who nodded at her as she walked past. She returned the gesture as she went to where she'd heard the screech of metal.

"Hello?" she called out. Okay, so now she was *literally* living a horror movie.

"Jilli?"

She took a step forward at the sound of Wes's voice and frowned as the sound of screeching metal echoed again, this time a lot closer.

"Don't—too late," Wes growled.

Her pulse raced, and she turned behind her to see the doors of the service elevator snap shut behind her.

"Well, fuck," Wes snapped and pulled her closer to him. Her hand instinctively went to the hard planes of his chest to steady herself, and she looked up at him, confused.

"What the hell, Montgomery? What do you think you're doing?" She tried to pull away, and his hands on her hips tightened for a moment before he let her go.

"You okay?"

"I have no idea? What on earth are you doing here, and what happened? Why were you holding me like that?"

There wasn't much light in the service elevator since they hadn't updated it yet and she could barely see him in front of her, but she did catch the slight blush to his cheeks when he answered.

"I got locked in here, and my phone doesn't work thanks to the metal of doom surrounding mè. I finally got the door open enough for me to get out, and then you walked right in and I couldn't let you get locked in, as well. So I followed you, intending to pull you out. But then the damn doors shut again." He pinched the bridge of his nose. "It's like a horror comedy of errors. It's a little ridiculous."

She blinked, not expecting that answer, and turned away from him to study the steel doors blocking their exit. Of course, that only made her think of the fact that there didn't seem to be an escape route, and they were now in a steel coffin, which was sucking up all the oxygen. Not to mention that the little light they had wasn't enough for them to study the mechanics of the damn thing. And, of course, she'd left her flashlight *and* her phone in the bag she'd left *outside* of the elevator. But if Wes's phone hadn't worked before so he could call someone for help, hers probably wouldn't have either.

No one would be able to hear them scream.

"Take a deep breath," Wes said softly, his arms around her again, keeping her in the present rather than the spiral of doom she knew she was cascading down. "There's an air hatch on top, so we can breathe all the oxygen we want. It also happens to have a metal plate in the center that makes it hard for people to hear us, but we *can* get fresh air in here. Just breathe, Jilli. You're doing fine."

Between his words and his arms around her, she could feel herself calming down a bit, and now she was embarrassed. She wasn't claustrophobic usually, but the memory of the metal doors snapping shut with such alacrity had made her panic slightly.

"Why do you call me Jilli?" she asked instead.

"I have no earthly idea." He chuckled roughly. The heat of his breath along her neck sent shivers down her spine, and she pulled away from him. They were in an odd situation with adrenaline going in too many awkward directions. There was no way she would do something stupid like enjoy being in his arms.

"We're only one floor up since the basement has access to this elevator, too. We should be fine, but let's try to get out of here nonetheless. Okay?" Wes said, his voice calm.

"Fine by me." She cleared her throat, ignoring the way Wes's gaze traveled over her. She hoped it was because he was checking for injuries, but from the heated way he stared, she had a feeling it wasn't that at all. "How did you get the doors open before? And, wait, I thought we had this checked out. Didn't we?"

He cursed under his breath. "Sheer determination and luck got the damn thing open before so we're going to have to try that again. And as for getting it checked out? Yeah, our inspectors did a full workup on it. Nothing like this registered for them. Everything was up to code, if a bit old. No idea what went wrong, but this is a lawsuit ready to happen." He gave her a look, and she narrowed her eyes.

"I'm not going to sue you, Montgomery. And once we get out of here, we'll just make sure no one gets on it again until someone can see what happened." She swallowed hard, sounding braver than she felt. Apparently, getting locked in a steel cage with Wes Montgomery was enough to make any woman edgy.

The elevator shook for a moment, and Jillian froze, her heart racing.

"We're fine," Wes said softly, though she wasn't sure if he'd spoken for her benefit or for his own just then.

She swallowed hard and took a deep breath once the elevator had been still for at least sixty seconds. "Um...let's get out of here."

Wes reached for her and tugged her close, their bodies pressed against one another as she tried to control her breathing.

"What are you doing?" she asked, confused by why he'd pulled her to him. She licked her lips, annoyed with herself for feeling any kind of attraction to him. It had to be the adrenaline of being stuck in a broken service elevator with him. Nothing else made sense.

"I...uh..." He let her go, shaking his head. "I was just making sure you weren't too close to the doors in case they opened again."

Okay, now *that* didn't make any sense, but she let him keep up with that lie since she didn't want to know what he was really thinking. Everything was already confusing enough without adding whatever was going on with them into the mix.

"Let's get to it, then," she said roughly, stepping away from him.

He frowned at her for a moment before getting to work on the doors. With the two of them pulling, they managed to at least get it open a couple of inches. However, there was no way she would be putting her hand or anything else through and risk losing it.

"Hey!" Wes called out. "Anyone still here?" He kept pulling on the door, and she did the same. His phone still didn't have any service, and she was just about to get worried when the doors snapped open.

She turned and met Wes's gaze before gripping his hand and running out of the elevator at full speed. Chest heaving, she went to sit next to her bag and let her head fall between her raised knees.

"Well..." She swallowed hard. "I wasn't expecting a panic attack."

Wes knelt in front of her, phone in hand. He didn't reach out and touch her, and for that, she was grateful. She wasn't sure she could handle that...now or ever.

"Do you need me to call someone?" He held out a bottle of water, and she took it from him, nodding her thanks.

"I'll be fine. It's not really a panic attack. I just needed to catch my breath since I still don't know what the hell just happened."

He sighed. "That seems to happen to us more often than not these days."

She looked up into his eyes and glared. They weren't supposed to mention what had happened before, and she'd been doing just fine living that way. "Anyway, I need to head out." She cleared her throat. "I have a date. With Clark." A second date, in fact, and she never had those.

Wes's eyes widened, and he stood from his crouched position, taking a step back. "Ah, well, I'll stay here and mark off the area before I call our engineer." He paused. "Have fun tonight."

She stood up and patted the dust off her pants. "Thanks. And, well, yay for not dying in an elevator shaft, am I right?"

He snorted and shook his head. "You're right about that. You going to be okay driving home?"

"I'll be fine. I just got a little overwhelmed for a second once the brevity of the situation hit me, but no worries. Are *you* going to be okay here alone?"

Wes shrugged. "I'm here alone all the time. I'm usually the first one on, last one off. It's sort of my thing."

Jillian couldn't help but smile at that. "You're more obsessive than I am about your job, and that's saying something. Anyway, I'm glad you're okay. I'll see you next week."

With that, she turned on her heel and did her best not to run out of the building.

Again.

CHAPTER SEVEN

W es gripped the steering wheel and tried to figure out just what the hell he was doing. Maybe getting stuck in the elevator just over an hour ago had stolen some of the oxygen from his brain cells and now he was making one poor decision after another.

After he'd watched Jillian drive away from the jobsite, confident that she would be okay—at least for the evening—he'd done what he said and called their engineer then blocked off the area in case any of his crew showed up before he did in the morning. Knowing his hours, it wasn't a high probability, but there was always a chance. Then he'd sent off an email to everyone letting the crew and the Montgomery Inc. staff know what had happened but leaving out mention of Jillian.

He honestly didn't know *why* he'd left her out since if it had been anyone else, he probably would have been specific, but he hadn't wanted to bring her into it in case some of the crew was like that recently fired idiot, Jeff. In a general memo, he hadn't needed to name names, but people would have started to gossip about who could have been trapped in the elevator. So, Wes had just put himself in the thing since he *had* been stuck alone at first. He just failed to mention that he'd trapped himself a second time with Jillian.

And that was just one more reason he needed to stay away from her because now, he was lying by omission in memos because he was afraid of what might happen if people started gossiping. And there would be gossip if they knew. In his opinion, construction sites were as bad as knitting circles when it came to gossip.

That should have been the end of his evening other than a cold beer and mindless television. But, of course, he made another mistake right after. As soon as he sent the memo from his tablet and headed to his truck, Sophia had called, wanting to see him. If he'd been in any other mood or hadn't just been stuck in a confined place with a woman he didn't want to want, one who clearly felt the same way about him, he might not have said yes.

Yet, here he was, in his truck, dressed in nice pants and a shirt after taking the quickest shower of his life and idling in a restaurant parking lot instead of doing something else he *should* be doing.

Wes looked up at the building in front of him and turned off his engine so he wouldn't waste gas. He'd been to this place a few times before with his family and once on a date with someone that hadn't led to anything serious, but that was it. It was a small French restaurant near downtown Denver but just outside it enough that it actually had parking. There was a valet service since the place edged on fancy, but he'd chosen to park in the back and ponder his life choices.

He'd never taken Sophia here, but she'd been the one to suggest this place. It reminded him of her tastes when they'd been together, and that worried him slightly. The food wasn't out of his price range, but it was a little steep for a date that wasn't a date.

Unless *she* thought this was a date and was back to her old ways of spending far too much money that wasn't hers.

"Stop it," he whispered to himself. He was already judging her, and he hadn't even seen her since she'd stopped by his house earlier. She'd told him that she was better, that she had gotten help and was stable, and he'd tried to believe her. It was just hard after everything she'd done to him—and herself for that matter—in the past.

He'd promised her that he would have dinner with her tonight, and he hoped he'd been clear when he said that it would only be *one* meal between friends. But now, he wasn't sure he'd been clear enough. She'd told him that she wanted more from him when she first saw him, said that she missed what they could have had if things hadn't fallen apart. But he *knew* that wasn't what he wanted.

Wes just couldn't quit her.

No, that isn't the right word, he thought to himself. He'd quit her before and had done his best not to think about her too often as he moved on. It was more that he couldn't stop wanting to make things better. He was a fixer. He *knew* that.

When Austin had found out that he was a father ten years into the game, Wes had wanted to fix that. He'd done his best to find out everything he could about the legal aspects and had called his friends who knew more than he did so Austin wasn't left alone dealing with everything on that end in addition to a new son and his then fledging relationship with

Sierra. And when Sierra had been hurt in the accident later on and then again when she almost lost the baby during delivery with Austin at her side, Wes had been there, as well, smoothing out as many details as he could on the everyday things so Austin and Sierra wouldn't have to worry about anything except their new family.

When his father had been diagnosed with cancer, like the rest of the Montgomerys, he'd done his research and tried his best to understand the disease that threatened his family. He'd done everything he could to make sure his mother had everything she needed while taking care of his father, yet Wes felt like he couldn't do much of anything at all. He'd felt hopeless in his life a few times, but that was one of the first times he'd truly felt like he could do nothing but pray that his father would make a full recovery.

When Miranda had been stalked and hurt by a man she'd only dated a few times, Wes had tried to step in like the rest of his brothers and fix everything he could. Of course, he hadn't been able to since she'd not only pushed them away but had also been able to lean on Decker while falling in love with him in the process. Wes had stayed on the sidelines, doing what he could to keep Miranda's ex out of the picture and had held her hand when she'd been hurt.

Wes hadn't been able to fix everything in his family's lives, but he'd done his best to keep trying. As Meghan's first marriage began to fail, he'd offered up his home to her and his niece and nephew to stay in, but his sister had refused. She'd let him help her find a place to live, but then hadn't let him help her with her small rental. He'd hated the place she'd been forced to choose, but she'd needed to do it on her own after her divorce. And when she finally found love again with Luc and things had almost gone to hell again, he'd held her hand while waiting in that damn hospital waiting room that seemed to have a Montgomery in it every month it seemed these days.

He'd tried to help his brother Griffin find his muse or whatever a writer needed in order to write, and had assisted the women of his family to hire Autumn. Wes hadn't been able to help much there, but he had been in the waiting room again when things turned violent with a man from Autumn's past.

Waiting rooms. He sighed. He spent so much of his life in them these days, he could count the tiles on the floor with his eyes closed.

All he did was wait. Wait and pray that he could find a way to fix things for everyone. Yet once again, he seemed to come up short.

He hadn't been able to fix Maya's heart when she fell for her best friend, Jake, and then fell again for Jake's ex, Border. He'd been forced to stand by and watch them work their way through their unusual and yet deeply rooted relationship themselves. He hadn't been able to fix a damn thing for them.

And then there was Alex and Storm.

Wes's grip tightened once again on the steering wheel as he closed his eyes, ignoring the sting that said he just might cry.

He'd failed Alex, and he knew it. He'd *known* his baby brother had a drinking problem, but he hadn't stepped in to help enough. He hadn't known everything was as bad as it ended up being, but he'd seen the signs and hadn't tried hard enough. It's possible Alex wouldn't have listened to him—he rarely did in those days—but Wes hadn't been able to help his brother stop hurting, and Alex had found a bottle instead.

As for Storm...well, Wes should have known his twin was hiding something from him. Maybe he had, and he'd ignored it because it would have been too hard to see that reflection inside himself, but he wasn't quite sure about that. Storm had been in pain not only physically but deep down in his soul, and Wes hadn't known.

Wes hadn't *known*.

Someone on the outside looking in might wonder why Wes felt the need to fix everything himself, but they didn't understand him. Of all his siblings, he was the most...stable. Nothing bad had truly happened to him. He wasn't hurt deep inside, and didn't have any scars that he tried to hide. He was just Wes.

Stable.

There.

And a fixer who couldn't fix what needed fixing the most.

If he couldn't use his stability and focus to help his family, then what good was it?

He shook his head, pushing those deep thoughts from his brain. Tonight, he was going to do something potentially idiotic and have dinner with a woman he didn't have feelings for anymore but had at one point. Because he wanted to help. That was it, he reminded himself. He would just have dinner, listen to what she needed to say, and then go home. He wouldn't put himself through a relationship with Sophia again.

And he wouldn't try to *fix* her.

Because, apparently, as much as he called himself a fixer, he wasn't any good at it when it came to the important things.

"And way to make everything about you," he said with a snort. He'd done his best to keep his family steady and do the little things in the background when he could, but as his thoughts rambled on, they had gone from helping to take out the trash to blaming himself for a disease he couldn't heal.

Good going.

He checked the time on his phone and cursed before jumping out of his truck. He'd spent a good ten minutes lamenting, and now he was running late. Sophia was probably already at the table wondering where he was. And where had he been? Right in the damn parking lot, brooding over things that were out of his control. Sure, that sounded like a great way to spend the evening.

He rolled his eyes and walked into the restaurant and up to the hostess station.

"Hello, how can I help you?" a pretty, young blonde asked with a wide smile.

"I have a reservation for two. Under Montgomery." Sophia had made the reservation under his name, and he wasn't sure how he felt about that. Not the fact that she'd made one, but that it felt as though she'd made one before he'd agreed to the dinner. Plus, she'd used his name and not hers, which he found a bit strange.

The hostess smiled again. "Yes, your other party is already here. Let me show you to your table."

Wes held back a wince. He hated being late, and tonight it was his own damn fault. *It has to be the elevator*, he thought with a held-back snort. That he was even on this date and then had spent far too long brooding in his truck—the damn thing had obviously messed up his brain.

Sophia sat at a small table near the front of the restaurant, her head down as she studied her phone and drank her sparkling water. She looked up as he approached and gave him her seductive smile, only he felt none of the attraction and spark he had all those years ago.

Sophia might be a different person than she was before, and that was honestly great for her, but he wasn't the same man either. He wanted nothing but the best for his ex, but he wasn't for her, and she wasn't for him. After tonight, he hoped she would see that.

"Wes, you're here."

He gave her a small smile as he took his seat. "I'm sorry I'm late." He took the offered menu from the waiter and nodded. "Thank you."

Sophia waved him off. "Oh, it's truly okay. I was just checking a few things on my phone, but now that you're here, I can put it away. How are you?"

"I'm good. How was your day?"

She shrugged. "I'm on vacation this week, but work never quite goes away, does it?"

He relaxed as they talked about work and nothing too serious, and for that he was grateful. When the waiter came over, they ordered their meals and continued their conversation as old friends, rather than the rising tension that would come from a date with a possible future attached to it.

"I'm glad I got to see you again," Sophia said as they finished their meals.

"Oh?" Wes asked, afraid of where this might be going.

She shook her head, her smile playful. "Because it tells me what I should have known before I showed up on your doorstep. What we had is in the past, and I shouldn't have come back to try and find it again."

He set down his water glass and frowned. "I agree with you. What we had is in the past, but I don't want to hurt you, Sophia."

She shrugged. "You aren't. I think I came here because I *thought* I'd find what I'm missing now. Or rather what I missed out on then. I'm not the same woman I was before, Wes, I hope you understand that."

"I'm beginning to," he said slowly, but before he could continue, the hairs on the back of his neck rose, and he turned to see Jillian and a man he didn't recognize walk into the restaurant.

That must be Clark.

Of all the places in all of Denver...

"Oh," Sophia said with a breathy laugh.

"What?" he said, turning back to her.

"Oh, nothing." A smile played on her lips again, and he didn't understand it, so he turned back to see Jillian and Clark coming toward them. As there was an empty table next to theirs, Wes knew exactly where the hostess was leading them.

Jillian's eyes widened when she caught sight of him, and she almost stumbled. Clark had his arm around her waist, and that seemed to steady her.

Wes would *not* be jealous.

"Jillian," Wes said as she sat down with Clark. "Fancy seeing you here."

"Wesley," Jillian clipped out. "I didn't know you'd be here either."

Sophia let out a small laugh, and Clark looked confused.

"Sophia, Jillian. Jillian, this is Sophia."

"Hello," Jillian almost bit out. "Wes, this is Clark." She waved over at him. "Wes is my boss."

Clark's posture relaxed marginally. "Ah. Nice to meet you."

"Likewise," Sophia put in.

Jillian's eyes narrowed as she seemed to recognize Sophia's voice from the phone call before. Oh, good, as if this weren't awkward enough.

"We're just about done here," Wes put in. "Enjoy your date." Had he put too much emphasis on the last word? Well, he hoped not because Jillian *should* enjoy her date.

And he'd go home alone.

Like he wanted.

Sophia gave him a knowing look, and he raised his hand, grateful when the waiter brought over their check right away. He quickly paid, doing his best to act like this wasn't awkward as hell as he ignored the couple seated far too close to him and listened to Sophia talk about her job as a sales rep.

They nodded at the other couple as they stood up to leave, and Clark waved at them. Jillian glared before nodding back, and Wes led Sophia out of the restaurant.

"Well..." he said, clearing his throat as soon as they stood outside.

Sophia tossed her head back and laughed, her soft brown curls falling down her back. "Oh, that was *so* interesting."

"No, it wasn't," he ground out.

"Wes, darling, it was, but I won't press. Thank you, though, for agreeing to come out to dinner with me. I know I'm not your favorite person in the world, but I do appreciate that you gave me the time to apologize." She leaned forward and kissed his cheek. "You're a good man, Wes Montgomery, and one day, I hope you find the perfect woman for you."

Wes frowned. "I..." He shook his head, not knowing what he was going to say. "I hope you find yours, too. Well, the perfect man I mean."

Sophia gave him a sad smile. "I hope I do, too, but as it turns out, I'm okay being alone. Who would have thought?"

And on that note, he walked her to her car and said goodbye. He didn't know if he'd ever hear from her again, and he was okay with that. They'd both grown since they were together, and he liked knowing she would more than likely be okay in the end. Of course, he couldn't quite get her last comment out of his head.

He was alone, too, after all.

Only he wasn't sure if he was okay with that. Yet he had no idea how to change it.

CHAPTER EIGHT

The next day, Jillian leaned against her kitchen counter and sipped at her iced tea. She had the whole day off, so instead of doing something fun like she probably should have, she'd cleaned her house from top to bottom. She'd even scrubbed the baseboards *and* the windows, so her body ached and she'd run out of cleaning supplies.

When she was stressed or worried, she either cleaned or worked. Since she now worked for a company that actually cared about its workers and overtime, she couldn't put in extra hours, so she cleaned.

A lot.

And now she had nothing else to do for the rest of the day to keep her mind off what had happened yesterday.

Thankfully, before she could go down yet another downward spiral in her thoughts, her phone rang. She smiled when she saw the readout even as her heart raced. It did that every time she saw her dad's name on her phone. While he used to call her often to see how she was doing or just to talk about their days, he did it more now, though he never said why.

They both knew why, though.

"Hey, Dad. How are you?"

"You know, you used to answer the phone with things other than asking me how I am." He paused, and she bit her lip, not wanting to say anything to upset him. "I miss those days, yet I'm glad I have a daughter who cares about me as much as you do."

And that was it. No more holding back the tears here.

"Don't cry," he whispered.

"I'm not," she said on a hiccupped sob. "No tears here," she lied. She cleared her throat and did her best to push away the bad thoughts that continually crept up to the back of her mind. "So, really, how are you?"

Her dad chuckled, and she couldn't help but smile at the familiar sound. "I'm good. Happy." He paused, and she wiped the rest of her tears. "Jilly-bean, I'm *happy*. I had a good day today and plan on having many more of them. Roger came over earlier, and we took a walk like the doctor wants me to. He'll be back later with his wife, Suzanne, for dinner. She made a casserole and wants to eat out."

They both laughed at that.

"Eating out means cooking it and eating at a neighbor's?" she asked, teasing.

"I'm not going to question things like that if it means I get her casseroles. You had Suzanne's food when you were little. Remember?"

Jillian nodded, then remembered he couldn't see her. "Yes, and from what I remember, they weren't all that low in fat and calories."

"Well, now, don't go ruining my evening. I'm making a salad on the side if that makes you happy."

She just laughed because she *knew* that salad would stay on the side the entire night and maybe get picked at. There was no way some lettuce, and maybe a sliced tomato if he was feeling feisty, could compete with Suzanne's casserole. Of course, now Jillian was hungry and knew she couldn't have anything like that if she wanted to be able to fit into her work clothes that week.

"I'm glad you have plans."

"And what about you? Have a hot date with that Clark boy? When am I going to meet him?"

Jillian held back a groan. Why had she told her dad about Clark? He'd bugged her about her dating life, and she'd mentioned a couple of weeks ago about her upcoming second date. She'd just done it to keep the attention off her, and now she regretted it.

"No plans other than maybe a hot bath tonight. Sorry to disappoint."

"And Clark?" he pressed.

This time, she did groan. "I'm no longer seeing Clark." There. That was honest and to the point.

Of course, her dad didn't let her stop there. "What happened? Did he hurt you? Do you need me to kick his ass?"

And this was one of many reasons she loved her father so much, even if she wanted to throttle him sometimes as any good daughter was prone to do. "He didn't hurt me, Dad. We just didn't work out. He was a nice guy but...well...he just wasn't for me."

Her dad sighed. "I'm sorry about that, Jilly-bean. I want you to be happy."

She trailed her fingers over the pattern on her granite countertops and shrugged though he couldn't see her. "I *am* happy." That much was the truth, but she wasn't going to lie and say she wasn't lonely.

"Then how about I say I want you to be happy *with* someone."

"I'm not going to stop dating completely. I'm just not going to see Clark anymore." Last night's date wasn't bad, but she hadn't been able to focus on the pleasant conversation once Wes and Sophia left. All she'd been able to do was imagine what the two of them were doing. Alone. Together. Sweaty and perfect for each other.

Jillian knew she wasn't frumpy in comparison but she sure as heck felt like it at that moment. Sophia had been all curves and sophistication with that smoky, sex-filled voice, while Jillian was all lines and awkwardness. Sure, she could do sexy when she felt like it, but as soon as she saw Wes with another woman, she'd felt so far from that it wasn't funny.

And, yes, it wasn't lost on her that she'd been on a date with another man and she'd been a little—make that *a lot*—jealous over Wes's date.

That was when she'd known that she couldn't lead Clark on. He was sweet and had a decent job and future in front of him, but he didn't make her swoon...didn't make her want to jump his bones every time she saw him. It wasn't fair to anyone when she had another man on her mind. Another man that apparently had another woman.

She held back yet another sigh.

Of course, she'd want a man that wanted another woman. That seemed to be her thing these days when it came to men, especially the Montgomerys.

"You there?"

She shook her head, clearing her thoughts. "Sorry, woolgathering. Speaking of wool, I'm going to go work on my knitting project so Meghan sees some progress. Adrienne is beating me as it is, and you know how I feel about losing."

"You're my daughter, after all," he said on a laugh. "I can't wait to see what you make me. Now go have some fun, baby girl. Love you."

"Love you, too, Dad." They ended the call, and she leaned back against the kitchen counter, that familiar feeling of loneliness settling over her. "Well, damn it." She really hated these pity parties of hers, and she needed to get over them and get on with her life.

On that note, she put away the remaining bottle of cleaning solution she had, wrote a grocery list for the next day since she needed more than cleaning supplies to get her through the week, got out a bottle of water from the fridge and her last apple, and sat down on her couch so she could get to work on her knitting project.

She just needed a cat, and she'd be the epitome of a single woman according to the media. And while she really wanted a new kitten or older cat to love and care for, she really wasn't home enough to start a pet's new life. Maybe she'd use some of her vacation days when and if she finally got a pet so she could be there for it.

And, yes, that seemed just about right. Taking vacation days so she could stay home with a cat. Such a thrilling life she had.

She turned on the TV to see what was on and ended up on an older James Bond film. A sexy man in a suit fighting bad guys with a smirk wasn't a bad way to spend the evening. She set her remote down and picked up her knitting, trying to remember where she'd left off on the scarf. She was only doing one kind of stitch and doing her best not to drop any. Of course, the hardest part for her so far had been casting on, and Meghan had helped with that. She wasn't sure she'd be able to do it herself when the time came.

As the movie progressed, she looked up every once in a while from her project, but since she had to watch her hands make each move at this point in her knitting career, she wasn't paying attention to the plot all that much. So, in essence, she was only looking up to see a sexy man in a dress shirt and pants.

And who did that remind her of? Along with that smirk, there was only one other person she thought of with a shirt like that and the muscles that lay beneath.

Wes freaking Montgomery.

With a scowl, she set her knitting down and picked up her water bottle, her throat suddenly felt parched as she thought about Wes and those damn muscles. Of course, her throat wasn't the only part of her on alert from the thought of him and how he'd felt beneath her hands when he pulled her close.

She let out a shaky breath and set her water down, her mind no longer on the movie or the knitting in front of her but on something—*someone*—she shouldn't be thinking about at all. Her nipples tightened, and her breasts grew heavy. She throbbed between her legs, aching.

"Damn it," she growled and quickly got up off the couch and stomped toward her bedroom. Well, if she was alone, apparently horny as hell, and only had one thing on her mind, she might as well give in to temptation and do something she knew was a very, *very* bad idea.

She pulled open the drawer on her bedside table and looked at her collection, trying to think about which one would suit her purposes for the night. Biting her lip, she pulled out the silicone dildo she loved and her vibrator that plugged into the wall and did amazing things to her clit.

If she were going to be bad, she was going to go all the way.

She could have lit some candles and put on music to make things sweeter, but Jillian didn't want anything sweet just then. Instead, she stripped out of her clothes and rolled her neck over her shoulders. Her body *ached,* and she knew that if she didn't come soon, she'd be on edge for the rest of the evening. Wanting to go even further, even though she was by herself, she bent over and pulled the nipple clamps out of her drawer. They were tiny ones that just circled the tip of her nipples that she sometimes wore under her bra because she liked the feeling and hadn't yet taken the plunge by piercing them. Maybe she'd go to Montgomery Ink finally and let them add permanent rings, but for now, these would do.

She slowly slid them over her nipples and tightened, the sting sending shock waves down to her clit. She swallowed hard, knowing she was already wet, *needing.* She quickly set everything else out and plugged in her vibrator.

As she settled herself in the middle of the bed, she reached for the lube she'd set out with her other things and slid her hand between her legs. She was hot and soaked, and just from the idea of what was to come.

She slowly teased herself with her finger, drawing small circles around her clit as her breaths quickened. Images of Wes came to mind, his head between her legs as she tangled her fingers in his dark hair. He'd lick and suck her, using that talented tongue on her until she came hard on his face.

She turned on the vibrator to low, resting it near her clit but not directly on it so she'd slowly rise along the crest. It set off a low hum, and she sucked in a breath, the vibrations rocking her but not quite high enough to make her come.

Now imagining Wes hovering over her, tugging at her nipples that mirrored the way her clamps worked, she arched her back and spread her legs. Her eyes still closed, she grasped around for her dildo and licked her lips before finally opening her eyes so she could lube it up. It wasn't too thick, but it was a pretty decent sized one, and though she was already wet and almost ready to come, she knew her body.

As she slowly inserted it inside, she moaned, the idea that the long, thick member was Wes and not an inanimate object almost sending her over. She put the vibrator back, this time directly over her clit at a slightly higher setting, and her hips shot off the bed, the sensations too much. She came hard, her body shaking as she imagined Wes making her come on the first thrust. Then she lowered her hips, held the end of the dildo and slowly worked it in and out of her, this time picturing Wes pumping his hips slowly, working them both up the wave once more.

She was almost at her peak again when the sudden image of Wes turning her over on all fours popped into her mind. Knowing she didn't have much time before she came again, she turned over, resettling her vibrator over herself and still working the dildo in and out of her. From this position, it wasn't easy, but the effort just made her hotter. Her nipples and face were pressed into her mattress as she panted, getting closer and closer. As soon as she imaged Wes's hands tightening on her hips as he slammed into her, she came again, this time, her hands dropping everything she was holding. A scream ripped from her throat as she panted, her body going hot and cold all over, the orgasm even stronger than the one before.

Soon, she found herself lying on her stomach, her dildo still buried inside her sensitive flesh as she pulsated around it, and her vibrator humming gently beside her hip, vibrating the mattress.

"Well, then," she muttered to herself, her bones feeling like jelly. She fumbled for the off switch and slowly pulled the thick dildo from her, once again imagining Wes doing that for her as he cleaned her up. Sadly, she was alone and had to clean up everything herself.

Blood rushed to her nipples as she undid the clamps, and she licked her fingers before rubbing out the sting. It wasn't the same as a man's mouth, but she sadly knew how to do what she needed to do on her own. She quickly cleaned everything up and hopped in the shower to wash off, determined not to feel guilty about what she'd done.

There is nothing wrong with a little fantasy, she lied to herself.

Wes was her boss. Her ex's twin, for freak's sake. She and Wes had decided not to do anything about the attraction burning between them, and she needed to get that through her skull. Having two freaking amazing orgasms while thinking about him would only confuse matters once she saw him at work.

Plus, he was probably with Sophia for the evening, and her thinking about him that way was wrong.

The idea of him and that other woman being together was like a cold splash of water over her, and she quickly hopped out of the shower and got dressed in comfy shorts and a tank without a bra.

No more thinking of Wes Montgomery. Ever.

And, of course, as soon as her phone rang in her bedroom, she *knew* who it was. Because her life sucked that way.

"Hello?" Did she sound as though she'd just come thinking of him while doing very naughty things to herself? She hoped not.

"Hey, Jillian. I was going over some paperwork and had a question. And now that I'm talking to you, I realize it's the weekend, and you're probably on your way out having a life...unlike me. I'll let you go."

"No, no, I'm home, too. Though I'm surprised you're not out with Sophia." She winced. Subtle, she was not.

Wes cleared his throat. "Sophia is an old friend." The way he said *friend* made her think there was more history than that, but she didn't say anything. "She was in town for a short while and wanted to catch up, but we're not...I mean...there's nothing..."

"You don't have to explain yourself to me," she said quickly, ignoring the relief rushing through her at his words. *Damn it, hormones, get a grip.*

"Ah, okay. Well, I guess I'm surprised you're not with Clark tonight?"

He'd phrased it as a question, even though it wasn't really one, and since they were both being idiots tonight, she answered him. "I'm not seeing Clark anymore."

"Oh." A pause. "Want to talk about it?"

She laughed. "Not in the least. How about you tell me about that paperwork?" There. That was professional. Right?

"Well, if you're sure you don't want to talk about Clark."

"I *really* don't want to talk about Clark."

"Okay, fine." He laughed, and the sound went straight to her core. Damn it, why did he have to do that? She was *not* falling for Wes or getting any of those tingly feelings she'd never felt for Storm. "What were you doing before I called?"

She blushed from head to toe. There was *no* way she was going to talk about that. Ever. "Knitting."

Wes laughed again. "Oh, right. Meghan said she was helping you and Adrienne learn to knit. Anything good yet?"

Jillian walked into her living room and sat down on the couch, thankful she'd turned off the movie before she went into her bedroom, and picked up her project. "Not in the least," she repeated. "I think I have one-eighth of a scarf, but it's sort of lopsided."

"I never had the patience for knitting," Wes said, surprising her.

"You knit?"

"Hey, guys knit."

"Of course, they do, but you? I can't see that." Of course, now she was picturing him concentrating hard on his project, and she couldn't help but smile.

"Yeah, I tried for a bit because it made Mom happy, but I'm too much of a perfectionist. Alex and Griffin were better than me, but I don't think either of them still does it. Austin was actually the best, now that I think about it. Those big hands of his move with surprising grace."

"Well, he *is* an artist." She'd never known that about the Montgomery men, and now she had a new respect for the matriarch of the clan.

"True, though Storm is one too in my opinion, and he never picked it up."

It was odd that bringing up the man that meant so much to them both didn't give her the same sense of awkwardness it used to when Wes talked about him. She didn't know what to make of that, but she knew it had to mean something.

"Well, I'm not that great of a knitter. Sadly, I don't know if I'll finish this project. It's pretty ugly."

"Keep going," Wes urged. "I always regret that I never finished mine."

That gave her an idea that made her laugh. "I have a deal for you. I'll finish mine if you try to do one, too."

Wes was quiet for so long she was afraid she'd moved too far from their antagonistic relationship. She didn't know what she was doing right then, but she couldn't help herself.

"You've got a deal," he said after a moment. "But you might need to help me."

Jillian played with a piece of yarn next to her. "Meghan would be better."

"True, but I don't want her to see how bad I am. What do you say?"

She let out a breath. "Okay."

"Okay."

The conversation moved on to work, and yet in the back of her mind, she knew something had changed between them. She didn't know what, but she had a feeling there was no going back.

The question was...did she want to?

And for that, she had no answer.

CHAPTER NINE

Wes looked over the progress at the bookstore the next Monday and couldn't help but smile at how far it had come in such a short time. The place had been gutted after the fire, and he knew Everly had lost any stock that hadn't been in the one closet in the back that had escaped damage. Insurance would cover most of it, but she'd never get those memories back.

Decker was in charge of this site with Storm overseeing more than he normally would since it was his fiancée's shop but Wes still came by often to see how things were going. It was important for him to remain on top of things for each project site, not just the ones he was the lead on.

"Did you see the floors Everly picked out?" Decker asked, walking up to Wes's side. "None of the hardwood or subfloors could be saved, so we're having to start from scratch, but the wide planks she chose are going to look nice in here."

Wes nodded. "Yeah, she sent over the link to the samples she'd chosen since she was so excited." He grinned. "The place is going to look kickass when we're done with it." At the moment, Everly was unemployed with two children who needed medical insurance, so they were working as fast as they could to get things up and running. He was pretty sure if they didn't stay on schedule, Storm would move up the wedding date before they hit any deadlines with the insurance companies. Luckily, though, everything was going smoothly so far—not that Wes would ever dare say that out loud. He wasn't about to tempt fate, not with his family's luck these days.

"How's the warehouse going?"

Of course, as soon as Decker asked that, images of Jillian popped into Wes's mind, and he did his best to hide his reaction to those thoughts. The fact that his reaction wasn't a scowl but something...*more* annoyed and intrigued him. When had she become someone he joked with and vowed to start knitting with? When had he started to crave her instead of thinking of her as the woman holding his brother back?

He'd been wrong in thinking that she was the reason Storm hadn't found his happiness, and for that, he would never quite forgive himself, but he still thought she was a pain in his ass. Much like she thought he was hers.

And yet they'd kissed.

They flirted.

They...talked.

And when they talked, she made him smile.

When on earth had that happened?

"Earth to Wes. You okay over there?"

Wes blinked and shook his head.

"What's wrong?" Decker asked.

"What? Oh, no, I was shaking my head to clear it, not to say no. Sorry, uh, what was the question?"

Decker raised a brow at him. "Okay, if you're not going to tell me why you're acting weird, I guess I'll just sic Miranda on you later."

Wes's eyes widened, and he held up his hands in surrender. "For the love of all that is good in the world, please don't do that. You know how she is."

"Yeah? Well, that's my wife you're talking about, so be careful what you say," Decker growled out.

"And that's my *sister*," Wes growled back.

The two of them glared at one another before breaking out in laughter. "Okay, then, Montgomery," Decker said with a grin. The man had been raised with the Montgomerys and was practically one himself. When he married Miranda, he'd actually taken her name rather than the other way around, and Wes couldn't help but love that. He was pretty sure if his parents had been able, Decker would have been adopted in years ago, though in retrospect, that was a good thing since it would have been awkward when Decker and Miranda wanted to get married. There were never any brotherly or sisterly feelings between them.

"Anyway, you were asking about the warehouse?" Decker nodded. "It's going good. The team is done with demo, thank the gods, but we're doing good with our schedule."

"Good to hear. I can't believe how big that project is."

"Yeah, it's our biggest. I just hope we don't screw it up." That was a common fear for him. He couldn't help it, it's just who he was. "Not that we're going to because, hello, we're Montgomery Inc. and we kick ass, but still, it's a lot of pressure."

"Pressure just eggs us on, right?" Decker asked, his smile widening. "Okay, I have to get back to work, but I wanted to check in on you. Need anything?"

Wes shook his head. "I need to head to the office and do some planning with Tabby since I've been out a lot lately on demo for the warehouse. You have anything you want me to drop off?"

"I'm good. I was at my desk this morning for like thirty whole minutes."

They both laughed at that. Decker hated sitting behind his desk when he could be working, but at his position, he needed a place where he could do paperwork and other things. Most of the higher ups in the company had a desk in their open concept office, but it was a rare day to find all of them there at the same time. That usually only happened on a really rough day of weather when none of them could work onsite.

Wes talked to a few of the crewmembers to see how they were doing but didn't keep them long since he didn't want to distract them or make them feel like he was micromanaging every move they made. He'd always hated when his dad stood behind him as he put up drywall. Yeah, his father had only done it to supervise or see if Wes needed anything, but it had always made him self-conscious, as both a son and a worker.

He waved at the crew as he headed out of the back entrance. The front was still blocked off from the public, and it was easier for him to get in and out that way. He still had to head to the office like he'd said, but now that he looked at the time, he was suddenly really hungry. Taboo, their family's favorite café that was owned and operated by a family friend and happened to share a door with Montgomery Ink, was close by. He figured he'd stop by there for lunch before going to the tattoo shop to say hello to Austin and Maya and the crew before he eventually went to the office. He had his tablet with him, so he'd be working the whole time anyway.

He shot off a text to Tabby to let her know what he was up to, then went through the side alley so he could get to the main street quicker. He stuffed his phone into his pocket and tightened the strap on his messenger bag that held all his things and whistled.

He almost didn't hear them come up behind him until they were right on him. He turned on his heel, then staggered back when the first punch hit him square in the jaw.

"What the hell?" He ducked under the next punch, but they outnumbered him three to one, and they'd blocked off the exits.

"Where is it?" the biggest one growled out.

He had no idea what the other man was asking, but he didn't have time to focus on it. They were on him again, this time using their fists and feet. Wes punched back, but only got one man in the cheek before he was down on the ground. He covered his head, trying to call out for help, then screamed as one of the guys stepped on Wes's hand.

There was a cracking sound, and then another guy punched Wes in the head so hard, he could only blink before he closed his eyes and started to fade. Quickly.

The last thing he heard was one of the men growling, "where is it?" once more.

Where was what?

Then nothing.

Wes blinked open his eyes, the blinding white above him making him groan. He quickly shut his lids and prayed that the splitting headache would just go away so he could sleep. Why did his head hurt like this anyway? Did he have too much to drink the night before?

Then everything came back to him with a hard slam to his chest, and he sucked in a breath. He'd been jumped in the alley. He'd tried to fight back, but he wasn't the best fighter, and he'd been sorely outmuscled and outnumbered.

"Wes? Go get the nurse. I think he's waking up."

Storm's voice pulled his eyes open again, and Wes let out a cough.

"Shit, you scared the crap out of me. Us. Miranda just ran out to get the nurse. We've been taking turns since there's so many of us and I think the sheer bulk of us started to worry some of the staff, so we're trying to keep quiet in our waiting room." His twin let out a snort. "*Our* waiting room. Hell, Wes, we have to stop doing this."

Wes blinked a few more times before narrowing his eyes at his twin. Storm never rambled like that, so Wes must have scared the crap out of him. "Seems to me, you were the last one in this bed."

Storm shook his head. "And I'd hoped I would be the last one to enter these halls." He sighed. "Well, technically, we're in a different hospital this time since you were found downtown instead of near where we all live."

"What happened?" Wes asked, his body aching. "And what's wrong with me?"

"Well, that's to the point. We don't know what happened. Decker found you in the alley, bloody, bruised, and unconscious. He didn't move you since it looked bad, or so he said." Storm let out a shaky breath.

"How did he know where to find me?" His pulse raced, and he did his best not to look down. His body hurt, and he figured he had a broken bone or two, but he knew as soon as he looked down, it would hurt more. That's how things had worked when he was a kid and scraped his knee, and he figured this would be like one big scrape.

"Tabby called Decker when you didn't show up and didn't answer your phone. She also called Hailey, Maya, and Austin because it was so unlike you." Storm cleared his throat. "Jesus, Wes. What the fuck happened?"

Wes started to shake his head then thought better of it. "I don't know. I got jumped."

"Fuck. I'm glad you're going to be okay because you *will* be okay, damn it. The cops will be here to talk to you soon, but we'll keep them back for as long as we can." His brother swallowed hard as the nurse walked in, Miranda on her tail. "Love you, man."

Wes must look like shit if Storm was getting so emotional. All the Montgomerys hugged and told each other they loved one another, but Storm was usually a little more closed off when it came to voicing his feelings. Even after falling for Everly, Storm was better at showing how he felt.

"Love you, too."

"Wes," Miranda whispered, tears falling down her cheeks. "I'm going to go talk to everyone outside while the nurse does her thing, but I love you, big brother. I don't like seeing you here."

"Love you, too, baby sis."

Storm wrapped his arm around her shoulder and led her out of the room, leaving Wes with the three nurses and the staff members who had shown up. Right as the door closed behind them, it opened again, and the person Wes figured was the doctor walked in.

She was an older woman with a kind face and strong hands—something he was grateful for since he was in a hospital after getting jumped.

"Well, Mr. Montgomery, it's good to see you awake. How about you tell me a few things as I check you over again and we can talk about the extent of your injuries." He appreciated her no-nonsense tone since he was starting to really freak out about what might be wrong with him.

She poked and prodded and made sure he knew his name before leaning back and tapping her pen on her folder.

"Okay, Mr. Montgomery—"

"Call me Wes."

She smiled then, just a quick one, but it relaxed him. "Okay, Wes. Here's the deal. You have multiple contusions and lacerations on your legs, arms, and face. All from what we figure were fists and kicks. You also have two bruised ribs, a slight concussion, and a very sprained hand. Not just your wrist, but every part of your hand. It's going to take a while to heal, and I'm pretty sure at some point you're going to wish it had just been broken instead of sprained, but you're going to be fine."

Wes let out a breath and finally looked down. As expected, the pain hit him hard, but knowing he wasn't hurt *too* badly made it slightly better.

He winced as he accidentally moved his left hand. Slightly.

"Your family said you were right-handed, so you can at least work behind your desk. No heavy lifting or strenuous activities for a while. I know you work in construction, but from what your family said, you can step back and oversee for a while as you heal."

"That's going to suck."

She laughed then. "True. I'm the same way when it comes to wanting to be in the thick of it, but you're going to have to follow my orders if you want to heal at a reasonable pace and not screw up your hand. Got me?"

He nodded, winced, then said, "Yes, ma'am."

She went over a few things, and the nurses did the same before she left him alone with a promise that the rest of his family would be in soon. Before he had a chance to close his eyes and rest his aching head, his family came in in pairs, each of them wanting to be close and make sure he would be okay. Only Jake was absent, as he had all the Montgomery kids at his place with his brothers and their wives helping out since there was no way he could handle everyone on his own.

Wes was just about to rest his eyes after Storm and Everly left when the door opened again, and Jillian walked through. He froze, and his eyes widened.

"Jilli."

She gave him a sad smile, frozen in the doorway. "I...I came in with Everly since we were at lunch when we heard. I wanted to make sure you had time with your family before I came back. I can go if you want to rest, though."

"Come here."

She swallowed hard, her pale face framed by her long, chestnut hair. Then she came to his side and sat in the seat the others had pulled up by his right side so they could see him better.

"I'm so sorry," she said, taking his hand.

"Why are you sorry? You didn't jump me."

She snorted. "No, I didn't. But I'm still sorry you're hurt. It's scary to see you like this."

It clicked then. "You're thinking about your dad. He's fine, Jillian. Right? I mean, his chest healed after that fall?"

She pressed her lips together, and he thought she might cry, but then she seemed to pull herself together. "He's okay. I was more worried about you, though. I don't like seeing you like this. How are you going to knit now that you can't use your left hand?"

He held back a laugh since his ribs really hurt. "It was all part of my plan."

She rolled her eyes, a smile playing on her lips though he knew she was still worried. "You could have just backed down from our deal. You didn't need to get beat up."

"Go big or go home, right?"

There was an awkward silence as the two of them stared at one another, their hands clasped. He honestly wasn't sure why they were like this with each other. They were barely friends, though he knew they were on a path to something that could be more, but they weren't there yet.

But no matter what was going on between them, there was one thing he *did* know. "I'm glad you're here."

Her face softened. "I'm glad you're glad. Just don't do this again."

"I'll do my best." They stayed that way for a while longer before two cops walked into the room to ask him questions. Since his father and Austin were with them, Jillian dropped his hand and stood to go.

"Heal, Wes. We can handle the warehouse." Jillian moved toward the door, and his gaze followed her.

"I'll try," he said honestly, knowing it would be hard not to want to help. But then there was nothing left to say on that as she left him lying on the bed, his body sore, and his mind and soul aching. His place in the world had been rocked more than once today, and he had no idea what any of it meant.

"Mr. Montgomery? Do you think you could tell us what happened?"

Wes turned to the others in the room and let his mind focus on them rather than whatever the hell was going on with Jillian. There would be time for that later, he promised himself.

What he'd do when the time came? Well, that he didn't know.

CHAPTER TEN

Jillian tapped her foot and glared at her dad. He licked his spoon and wiggled his brows before going in for another bite of gelato.

"Dad..."

"Sorry, can't hear you. I'm too busy salivating over this butter pecan." He took another bite and groaned. She did her best not to laugh at the look of pure bliss on his face but couldn't help it. He just looked *so* happy with his formerly confiscated gelato.

"The doctor said you need to watch your sugar."

"I know. I was there, remember?" He set the spoon in the sink and went to put the pint in the freezer. So he wouldn't have to bend down and pull at the handle, which sometimes was a little too hard for him, she took the pint away and put it in the freezer herself.

"Since you were there and know, you shouldn't be so cavalier about it."

As soon as she stood up, he rested his hand on her shoulder and gave it a squeeze. "I had three bites, which I'm allowed, Jilly-bean. It's okay. Really. And at least it was the organic kind without any of those nasty chemicals inside that could make things worse."

She winced and leaned forward so she could give him a hug. "I'm sorry I'm a menace. I just worry."

"You wouldn't be my daughter if you didn't worry." He kissed the top of her head, and she sighed into him. "It was good gelato."

"It's my favorite brand for a reason," she said with a soft laugh. "So, what's on the agenda for the day? I figured we could go see a movie or maybe go for a drive up into the mountains."

"I think a drive would be nice. Roger is coming over later this afternoon to watch the game, so nothing too crazy."

It was still early, and they could do a short drive at least into the foothills and get some lunch on the way back without tiring either one of them out. With her workload these days and the fact that she didn't sleep well thanks to dreaming of a certain Montgomery and what could have happened if Decker hadn't found him, she tired easily. Her hands shook, and she clenched her fists to hide her reaction. Her father knew what had happened to Wes since she'd told him, but she hadn't mentioned that she'd stayed in his hospital room for so long and had waited with Wes's family for hours to hear news.

She'd seen the way the others had looked at her while they waited, but there hadn't been anything else for her to do. She'd been with Everly when Storm called the other woman, and she hadn't thought twice about going to the hospital with her. Everly's boys had been at day camp, and that meant Jillian and Everly could go right to the hospital to meet the Montgomerys.

Most of them had looked surprised for a moment when they saw her walk in, and then it was as if she were supposed to be there all along. She'd learned through Storm over the past few years that this wasn't the first time the family had met in a waiting room around the city's numerous hospitals, but this *had* been the first time they were waiting to hear news on Wes.

When she and Everly arrived, Storm had opened his arms to the both of them. For a moment, it had seemed a bit odd to hug her friend who happened to be her ex at the same time as his fiancée, but in reality, they had all moved on to the point where they were just friends and lived their lives. Storm was hurting because of what was going on with his twin, and that meant that Jillian would be there for him.

And, of course, she had also been worried beyond reason about Wes.

Jillian still couldn't believe that he'd been jumped so close to the bookstore and where most of their friends worked. Whoever had attacked him hadn't wanted money since they had left Wes's wallet behind untouched, so they still didn't know why he'd been jumped as he had. But she knew she'd never get the image of him lying in bed, bruised and exhausted, out of her mind, no matter how many times people told her he would be okay.

It had been almost a week since the incident, and he was just now able to walk around easily and oversee the project site. She'd taken the day off to hang out with her dad since she had an overabundance of vacation days already and hadn't actually gotten that kitten she'd been thinking about.

And if she let herself, she'd spend the entire afternoon wondering why she'd reacted the way she had when she visited Wes in the hospital. She couldn't believe she'd held his hand for as long as she had and hadn't cared if anyone else saw her.

He was just her boss. She had to keep reminding herself.

Only she knew he wasn't merely her boss. What that *more* was, she didn't know and wasn't sure she could let herself figure out. So, instead of continuing to dwell, she'd spend the day with her father and ignore whatever feelings kept bubbling up inside of her.

"You're thinking too hard again," her dad said softly. She looked up to see him staring at her, and she smiled brightly, hoping it didn't ring too false. "Let's pack up some water and snacks for our drive." He winked, and she laughed for real this time.

"You *just* had gelato at nine in the morning, Dad. Snacks?"

"What's a road trip without snacks?" He waggled his brows and moved back so he could turn toward the refrigerator. She snorted and followed him, frowning when her phone buzzed in her purse on the counter.

"Answer that," her dad said when she didn't move toward it.

"I have the one person I want to talk to today right here. Anyone else can wait."

Her dad shook his head. "It could be Wes."

She froze. "Uh...why would that matter?"

"I wasn't born yesterday." He raised a brow, and she wanted to curl in on herself like she was a little kid. "I've seen the way your eyes either light up or glare when you talk about him. And he was hurt recently, so go answer to see if he's okay."

She sighed and went to her purse, annoyed that her father could read her so well. "It could be someone else." Of course, it wasn't. "Hello, Wes." She held back a laugh as her father gave her a look of superiority.

"Hey, can you come down to the warehouse? We need you ASAP."

She frowned. "I took today off for a reason, Wes."

"I know, and I feel like shit for asking you to come in, but we have a leak that the city fucked up on, and if you don't come down now to fix it, we'll be weeks behind. I know we're in the middle of hiring help for you, but we're not there yet. Do you think you can come in? We really need you."

"Go," her dad said. "We can do the trip this weekend if the weather holds. We have time."

She let out a shuddering breath, annoyed that she had to choose at all. Her father might say they had time, but ever since the diagnosis, she didn't feel as if they had *enough* time.

"Do you have an appointment with your dad today? Hell, I'm sorry, Jilli. I'll figure something out. There's another plumber I can call to see if they can work on a contract basis today."

She was already shaking her head and giving her dad a hug as Wes spoke. "I'll be there, Wes. But we *need* to get me help because I can't do this all the time."

"I know. We're working on it. It's been one set of annoying circumstances after another, but I truly appreciate it." There was yelling in the background, and Wes cursed. "Thank you. Seriously. Thank you, and tell your dad I'm sorry. I have to go."

"See you in a bit," she ground out, pissed off that she had to go to work on a day she had specifically taken off to spend with her father. And while she knew the Montgomerys would honor that request in any other case, it still sucked that she had to go in because of someone else's mistake.

"Love you, baby." Her dad hugged her tightly and kissed her forehead. She closed her eyes, tears welling because of her anger and just the idea of leaving her dad today when she didn't want to.

"Love you, too," she choked out. "I'm sorry I'm ruining our day."

He leaned back and cupped her cheeks. "I have my moments with you every day. I'll see you when you're done. It's an honor, isn't it? That the Montgomerys think you're so amazing at your job that they can't work without you."

"You say that, and later I'll feel proud, but right now, I'm just annoyed."

"You're my kid, of course, you're annoyed." He kissed her temple again. "Now go kick butt and let me know how it goes. Love you, Jilly-bean."

She laughed and pulled away. "Love you, too, Dad."

She hugged him one more time and grabbed her things so she could head to the site. Today was just one more example of why she needed help, and they all knew it. The company used to have four plumbers, but two of them had moved away, one had retired, and they'd fired the other.

There was a shortage in the area at the moment since the housing boom had slowed and everyone was for one reason or another starting up their own companies and overcharging. But Wes and Storm had hired four more people to work under her—only they had to go through recertification and wouldn't be able to start for another week or two. It was the company's policy, and she had gone through it, as well, but the timing sucked.

Honestly, she'd been lucky that they'd tried to give her a day off at all and *knew* they would have honored it if things weren't so crazy, but it still annoyed her that she had to come in when she'd wanted to spend the day with her father. Add that to the fact that she still felt weird when she was around Wes, and it made for an uncomfortable situation altogether.

She let out a breath as soon as she pulled into the parking lot and turned off her engine. People were milling about and weren't running in panic, so she took a few extra minutes to center herself. For some reason, every time she was with Wes and even the slightest annoyed, her temper blew. Okay, so she knew the reason, and it had everything to do with the burning attraction between them. The fact that they both actively ignored it—or at least tried to—didn't help her temper. Nor did it help his, since she wasn't the only one with a short fuse when they were near each other. But no matter that her body burned when she was near him, nothing could change between them. She might not be going on another date with Clark, and Wes had said Sophia was just an old friend, but that didn't mean they could have each other.

It just wouldn't work out and would make things harder with her working for him and with the fact that she was still friends with Storm and learning her relationship with Everly. It was all so complicated and borderline soap opera, that she knew the best thing for everyone was for her and Wes to stop flirting or whatever the hell they were doing. No more stolen glances. No more phone calls about knitting bets and explanations about who they were dating. Just no more Wes.

So, of course, she jumped and let out a squeal when Wes tapped on the window of her truck with his good hand. His bruises and cuts were healing, but he still had more healing to do.

"Jesus," she gasped before grabbing her bag and opening the door. "You scared the crap out of me."

He held up his hands—one still in a soft brace that made her wince inside—and raised his brows. "I didn't mean to. You were so lost in thought or whatever, I wanted to make sure you were okay. You *are* okay, aren't you?" He looked genuinely sincere and worried about her, and that just mixed up her already tumultuous emotions. She didn't want him to care about her. She couldn't deal with the fact that Wes was just a good guy who cared about a lot of people. She needed him to be standoffish and make it easy for her to stay away from him and keep him out of her thoughts. She needed to stay mad when it came to him so she could keep her distance.

She needed to remember that she was pissed off that she had to work today and, somehow, it was going to be all Wes's fault. And if she kept up that internal dialogue where she sounded like an insane person, maybe she'd get over her attraction to this particular Montgomery.

"I'm not okay, actually," she bit out. "I shouldn't have to be here because someone else screwed up and because your company can't keep a plumber. Just because you can't deal with timelines and organization, doesn't mean I have to ruin my plans." She was so off base, it wasn't funny, but everything came out as a growl instead of a legitimate complaint. It honestly wasn't the Montgomerys' fault that this happened, yet she was putting it all on Wes's shoulders.

From the narrowing of his eyes, she knew he didn't appreciate it. "You were told that you might be called in, Jillian." His tone was frosty, and it only put her back up. "You were told that this wasn't the best time to take a vacation day but that we would do our best. You were *told* that you would still be on-call like every single person in your place in the hierarchy of this company at this stage in the project. That means Meghan, Luc, Decker, Tabby, Storm, and I are here to clean up a mess not of our making. You are part of that hierarchy, even if you think yourself better than us. Now, if you're done acting like someone not of your level in your profession, I will show you where we need you."

He raised his chin, and she met his gaze.

Damn it.

She hadn't meant to sound like a bitch, and now she was embarrassed and pissed off at the same time. Thankfully, there was no one else near them to hear their conversation, but there was no denying the tension in their postures. It seemed no matter what she did, she'd always be fighting with Wes Montgomery—even if she thought they'd been on a path to something far calmer. Or maybe that was the problem. They *hadn't* been on their way to something easier, but rather something a whole lot more complicated.

"Show me where you need me," she said slowly, her tone neutral. She was *not* an asshole, and she needed to remember that. They could fire her for her attitude, and with the way she constantly butted heads with Wes these days—playful phone conversations and the holding of hands at hospitals aside—he was still her boss.

"Right this way," he said after a moment of studying her face. She followed him after she'd picked up her heavy toolkit. She was grateful that he didn't offer to help pick it up and carry it for her. The only person who had tried doing that on the Montgomery crew had been Jeff, but his offer had come with a leer and lewd remarks. If she needed help, she'd have asked, and off the job, any of the Montgomerys would have offered. They kept the lines clear between friendship and profession, and she needed to do a better job of that herself.

With Wes by her side, she got to work and did her best to clean up the mess left by the city and poor planning from the previous owners. It was a messy job, and one she wasn't in the mood to do, but in the end, when she was able to actually help out and *fix* things, she got that buzz of adrenaline that told her she'd picked the right line of work. There were just some things she could do that others couldn't, and *that* was why she kept doing it.

About four hours into her workday, her phone rang from her bag, and she frowned. It wasn't her dad's ring, and she didn't know who would be calling her today since it was technically still the middle of a workday, but she went to answer it after quickly drying off her hands.

Wes stood up with her and pulled out two bottles of water, tossing one at her as she reached for her phone. She caught it and rolled her eyes since he had been far closer to hitting her in the shoulder than actually giving her water.

The readout on her screen made her freeze, all thoughts of levity falling away.

"Roger? What is it?" She was surprised how calm she sounded, though she was anything but calm.

Wes must have heard something in her voice, though, because he set his water down and tugged her bottle from her hands, setting it next to his. He stood by her, hovering with his hands on his hips as she blinked at Roger's voice.

"Jillian, honey." Her father's neighbor didn't say anything else, and she let out a shaky huff of breath.

"What's wrong, Roger? Are you with Dad? Why isn't he calling me?" Her voice was edging on hysterical, and she knew it, but she didn't care.

"I came over to watch the game, and your dad didn't answer the door or his phone when I tried calling him. You gave me a key, remember? In case I needed to get inside in case of an emergency? So I used it and walked inside."

He was silent for another stretch of breaths, and her hand shook.

Wes stood closer, questions on his face, but she couldn't see anything beyond that. It was as if the world had gone into a tunnel and the only thing she could see was Wes's face, the only thing she could hear was Roger's breathing on the other end of the line.

"I thought he'd fallen asleep in that big chair of his with a blanket tucked over his lap. I would have left then, thinking I'd just interrupted his nap, but I wanted to make sure he was okay."

Her legs shook, and Wes put his hand on her hip, steadying her.

"Roger..."

"He's gone, honey. He wasn't breathing when I went to him, and I called 911. They pronounced him dead on scene." He choked out a sob, but Jillian only blinked, the stinging behind her eyes blurring her vision. "The coroner is on his way to pick him up to take him wherever they take him. I don't know anything else, Jillian. You need to come home. I...I don't know what to do, darlin'. I'm so damn sorry. I'm so damn sorry."

He started crying then, big sobs that she knew would shake his large frame and would be heard from miles away, but she could only hear them as a bare whisper.

"I...I'll be right there." She hung up, not knowing what else to say. She couldn't find the words to tell Roger that it wasn't his fault, couldn't find the words to say everything would be okay and that he didn't need to cry.

It was all a dream, right?

She'd just left her father smiling and laughing in the kitchen. He'd stolen bites of gelato for fuck's sake. He was *fine*.

Her father was *not* dead.

"Jillian? What's wrong? Talk to me."

Wes stood in front of her, his warm hands on her upper arms as he bent so they were eye level.

She should have been with her father.

She shouldn't have been here.

She could have helped.

She could have done something.

She...she couldn't think.

Tears fell down her cheeks, and she heard a keening wail that echoed throughout the large warehouse. For a moment, she wondered where that sound had come from until she realized that it was her.

The tightness in her chest was real, and the salt on her lips and tongue was from her. Wes pulled her close, holding her to his chest as she sobbed and fought for breath. She couldn't tell him what was wrong, couldn't yell at him for making her be here.

Because it wasn't his fault.

It was hers.

She hadn't been enough.

She hadn't been able to keep her father here.

And now, he was gone.

And she was alone.

Again.

CHAPTER ELEVEN

Wes tugged at his tie, grateful that he could forego the brace for now, and wondered how on earth all of this had happened. One moment, he'd been fighting with Jillian; the next, working side by side and getting the job done. And then...well, the next thing he knew, her world had shattered, and he hadn't known how to pick up the pieces. Hell, he didn't even know if he had the right to try.

Ashton Reid was dead.

He'd died of a heart attack peacefully while he napped in his favorite armchair. He'd been a tough and strong man throughout his life until one fall had exacerbated the symptoms he'd been ignoring for far too long. If he'd survived the heart attack, he'd have faced a slow and agonizing recovery as his body would never be truly strong again with the onset of his Parkinson's.

And Wes had forced Jillian to come to work instead of being by her father's side. He'd never forgive himself for that. Of course, he *knew* there was nothing she could have done, and it probably would have been worse for her if she'd been the one to find him, but she'd lost those hours with her father because of him.

Most of the Montgomery clan would be at the funeral, though Autumn and Griffin were staying at Wes's parents' house with all of the children. Autumn and Griffin might not have children of their own, but they helped to raise the latest generation and were there when anyone needed them. The rest of the family wanted to be there for Jillian even if some of them only knew her in passing. But ever since Storm had introduced her to them as his friend, and she'd started working for the company, the Montgomerys had done what they did best and adopted her.

They wouldn't let her do this by herself.

Whatever *this* was.

He rubbed his fist over his chest, that aching numbness settling in. He couldn't imagine what she was going through, even though he'd almost gone through it himself just a short time ago.

When Harry Montgomery was diagnosed with cancer, Wes had thought his entire world had shifted beneath his feet. Though the prognosis had looked good according to the doctors, nothing was ever set in stone, and there was a reason prostate cancer was a leading cause of death in men his father's age.

He'd almost lost his dad to a disease that had ravaged his body, but in the end, Wes had been lucky. Jillian was not.

He closed his eyes, swallowing the bile in his throat. He couldn't help but look at the similarities of their situations and the vast, cavernous differences. And because he was a tiny bit selfish, he knew he'd hug his father close today, grateful that he was still with them even as Wes mourned alongside Jillian.

Storm had been the one who knew Ashton. He had met the man a few times and had gotten to know him over the years. Wes had no connection to the man who had raised Jillian beyond that he had seen and respected the beautiful and strong woman Ashton had raised alone.

He had no idea if Jillian's mother would attend, and didn't know the entire backstory other than Storm's mention that the older woman had left early on in Jillian's life and never returned.

He'd never forget the sound of Jillian's grief when she'd fallen into him after hearing about her father's death. He'd never forget the weight of her sorrow on his chest as she'd tried to compose herself and failed.

Storm had been the one to drive her to her dad's place with Wes following behind in his own truck so his brother wouldn't be stranded. Wes had carried her to Storm's truck in silence and hadn't said a word as he stood behind his twin on her porch. She'd waved them off, telling them she could handle everything on her own as Ashton's neighbors had been near, and Wes had finally let Storm pull him away.

There had been nothing they could do, and he'd known Jillian didn't want them to see her broken like she was. It had taken all within him not to pull her close and never let her go. The fact that he'd felt that at all told him he'd been burying his feelings for this particular woman for far too long, but there was nothing he would or *could* do about it now.

"Enough," he whispered to himself. "Enough."

He quickly picked up the rest of his things, grabbed his keys, and headed out to his car. He had a truck for work and weekdays, and a black BMW that he tried to use on the weekends. He had decided that today was the day for the dark-tinted windows of his car and not the loud engine of his truck. He was in his mid-thirties without a wife and kid and had held a steady, well-paying job for over a decade. He'd indulged in his car and the land surrounding his home since he didn't have much else in his life.

The idea that he would be coming home alone after the funeral bothered him. Somehow, so much of his life had passed him by while he was focused on his job and his family. It was as if he'd forgotten to make and live his own life beyond that.

It was odd how death could remind the living that they still needed to live.

Wes was quiet on his drive to the cemetery, deciding to not even turn on the radio for the background noise of music. They were doing a graveside service and a wake at Ashton's favorite pub. Wes hadn't been to many funerals in his life—luckily—but he knew that while people would want to make the wake a celebration of life, it would still be a somber occasion for those the man had left behind.

In particular, the daughter who remained.

He pulled into the parking lot and shut off his engine, his hands shaking a bit. He had no idea how he could help Jillian today, but he knew he had to try. If she needed someone to yell at, to punch and hit until her pain eased, he'd be that person. If she needed him to go away and not look at her, he'd do that, too. If, for some reason, she wanted him to hold her and keep her close, he'd do that gladly.

He just knew he had to do something.

Wes met the rest of his family on the edge of the crowd that had come to celebrate the life and mourn the death of Ashton Reid. The proceedings hadn't started yet, though Jillian was in the middle of the large crowd of people who had known the older man. She looked so alone in the crowd of mourners who were much older than she and looked as if they didn't know what to do with her.

"Come on," Wes's mother whispered, tugging at his arm. "Harry, get Storm and Everly. We're not letting that girl do this alone."

And that was his mother in a nutshell. Even as emotion clogged his throat, he knew there would never be another person in his life or on this earth quite like Marie Montgomery.

The rest of his siblings and their spouses went to take seats scattered around the back as there were never enough chairs for all of his family to sit together, while Wes, his parents, and Storm and Everly went up to Jillian's side.

Her eyes widened a moment when she saw them before she gave them a sad smile that seemed to reach her eyes.

"You came," she whispered, though her eyes were for him and him alone before she turned to his mother. "Thank you so much for coming."

Marie framed Jillian's face with her hands and leaned close, resting her forehead on hers. "Of course, we did. We love you, darling."

Jillian blinked away tears before closing her eyes tightly as she leaned into his mother's embrace with his father by their sides, his hands on each of their shoulders. "I...thank you."

Everly and Storm went next, each hugging her tightly before stepping back, leaving a space for Wes to move forward. He didn't know why his mother had chosen him to come with her, other than the fact that his mom seemed to know everything before anyone else did. But now, he was glad he was there—even if it was a bit awkward.

"Jilli," he whispered.

Her lower lip wobbled, but the tears didn't fall this time. "Wes."

He held out his arms, and she sank into his hold for a deep hug that lasted only a few seconds before they each pulled back, equally confused and conflicted at what was going on between them.

Jillian turned to his mother, her hands clasped in front of her, and lowered her voice. "Can you sit with me?" she whispered, her cheeks red. "I...I don't have anyone else."

His heart tore in two, and it was all he could do to keep from reaching out and holding her close again.

But before he did something as stupid as that, his mother kissed Jillian's cheek and nodded. "Of course, baby. Of course. Why don't you take your seat, and Harry and I will take these two."

As there was only one empty spot left, Storm and Everly hugged Jillian again before going back to the rest of the family, leaving Wes to awkwardly stand with his hands in his pockets. His mother gave him a stern look, and he nodded, pulling himself out of his fog as he walked up to Jillian.

"Come on, Jilli, I'll be right beside you the whole time." He wasn't sure that would be a comfort, but when she let out a sigh and met his gaze, he knew he'd done the right thing.

"Thank you." Her words were barely audible, but he'd heard the emotion behind them.

He took her hand and sat down with her, his parents sitting next to him. He hated the fact that Jillian had been alone until the Montgomerys showed up. Yes, she'd had her father's friends, but from the way she'd set herself apart in the sea of people, he'd known they hadn't been *her* friends.

He gave her hand a squeeze, and her grip tightened. She kept her gaze straight head as the pastor came forward to speak about Ashton and the bright light he'd been. Others sobbed quietly behind him, while some sniffed or coughed, emotion filling the small tent that covered them and blocked them from the sun.

Jillian didn't cry at the man's words; instead, she stared blankly ahead, her breaths shallow as she held onto Wes's hand, her grip tight. Because he was so focused on her, he didn't listen to what the officiate was saying. He knew Ashton deserved more, but he could only keep his attention on the woman at his side and make sure she didn't feel alone.

Soon, the man finished, and they started the next stage of the service. Wes stood up with Jillian and then took a step back so she could go to her father's graveside. She placed her hand on his casket and lowered her head before letting out a shaky breath and turning away so she could let the others mourn, as well.

She was so damn strong.

He said his goodbyes to a man he'd never met but had admired because of the woman he raised, before standing off to the side with Storm and some of his other family. The women had gone to help Jillian, but Wes knew having him around would only stress her out. He wasn't sure *how* he knew that, but he did.

"Do you know who they are?" Storm asked quietly, nodding toward a group of large men in suits who had set themselves apart from the rest of the group and studied the mourners from behind dark glasses.

"No," Wes answered, though he wasn't sure what made him feel a bit off when he looked at the other group of men. "I didn't know Ashton, though. Could be some of his friends."

"They didn't sit with the rest of us," Austin said with a shrug. "But not everyone mourns the same way."

Wes nodded before turning back to Jillian, putting the men in suits and dark glasses out of his mind. He wouldn't go to the wake, he decided. That would be a time where people would tell stories of Jillian's father and want to mourn in a setting where they were comfortable. He knew Storm, Everly, and his parents would go for Jillian, but he didn't feel like it would be his place.

Jillian looked up at that moment, her gaze meeting his before she turned away as someone came up to her to speak.

"You want to tell us what that's about?" Storm asked quietly.

"Not the right time or place." Wes didn't look at his brother or the rest of the Montgomerys around him. He wasn't sure what they'd see when they looked into his eyes as it was.

No one said anything else after that, and the crowd slowly dispersed as they went their separate ways. Wes stood alone in the cemetery for longer than he probably should have while those that worked for the funeral home went about their business.

He had a lot to think about, but couldn't quite get his thoughts together to figure out what everything meant.

Soon, he told himself.

Soon, he'd figure out what it all meant and what was going on inside him. First, though, he would make sure Jillian could mourn. And throughout it all, he'd be what she needed him to be.

What that was, well, that was something he needed to figure out.

Soon.

CHAPTER TWELVE

"**A**re you fucking kidding me?" Jillian growled and threw her wet towel on the ground, knowing it wasn't going to sop up any of the water that had already spilled on the cement in front of her. "What the hell, you goddamn thing? Why won't you bend to my will and do what I damn well need you to do?"

It had been two weeks since she'd laid her father to rest, and since then, she'd apparently lost all her drive and skill when it came to plumbing. The prime example for the day was the fact that she couldn't fix her *own* water heater.

She didn't need to replace the sucker, she knew that much, but it was unwilling to cooperate and let her fix it.

The bastard.

Knowing if she didn't back away from her traitorous appliance, she'd throw something or break it even more, she picked up her tools, made sure the main water was off, and went back upstairs. It wasn't as if she could call a plumber to help her—not even one of the guys Wes and Storm had hired to work under her.

She hadn't taken time off and didn't want to, so she'd been able to help train them the way she wanted the guys to work with her. So far, they hadn't acted as if they cared that it was a woman telling them what to do, so she counted that as a plus.

That was about the only win in her column these days.

Every morning, she got out of bed, showered, and did her normal routine in a world that felt anything but normal. Then she'd go to work, do what she thought she did best, and only talk to those who needed direction. She did her paperwork on time and nodded along when others asked how she was doing.

She was alive, but she wasn't living. Wasn't feeling.

How was she supposed to feel when she couldn't hear her father's booming laugh? How was she supposed to know that everything would be okay one day when she *knew* it couldn't be without her dad hiding gelato or wanting her to finish knitting him a scarf?

She hadn't looked at her knitting bag since the funeral.

She didn't know if she ever would again.

What was the point?

There were still the legal matters of her father's home and estate to deal with, but when he'd been diagnosed with Parkinson's, they'd gone to a lawyer together and had set up as much as they could ahead of time. She'd thought they'd still have years before she had to deal with any of that stuff. As it turned out, she only had a few meager months.

She'd never gotten her road trip.

Never got to walk through the foothills with her father as he told her stories from when she was younger.

She hadn't finished going through old boxes that her father had set out for her so they could remember happier times.

And she hadn't heard from her mother once since she left a message on the woman's voicemail. Jillian hadn't been surprised, but she was still hurt and pissed off.

Apparently, Boca Rotan and her mother's new children were far more important than the man she'd once claimed to love and the child that had been born from that love before being left behind. The woman had *married* her father. She'd had a child with the man and hadn't bothered to send flowers or even text Jillian back saying something like she was sorry for her loss.

Anything would have been better than this silence.

Of course, as soon as Jillian thought that, she figured if she *had* heard from her mother, that would have stirred a whole other set of emotions within her.

And she knew she was focusing on her job and the lack of communication from her womb donator because she didn't want to look too closely at the fact that she'd lost a part of herself when her father died.

Somehow, she was a mixture of numbness and heightened emotion, and she had no idea what to do next except remember to breathe and take one step after the other.

Hell, she'd never felt so out of sorts. So freaking *lonely*.

Maybe she would get that kitten, after all.

Before she could get any more introspective, her doorbell rang, and she frowned, wondering who could possibly be at her door.

When she opened it, however, she should have known who was there. "Wes." She swallowed hard, still not used to why she reacted the way she did whenever she saw him. Her heart raced, and her knees shook ever so slightly.

He made her feel when all she wanted to do was remain blissfully numb.

"Hey." She watched his throat as he swallowed hard before stuffing his hands into his pockets. "I just...well, its Sunday, and I figured since I'm off for the day, I'd come by and see how you were. Though now that I'm here, I think I made a mistake."

"It's Sunday?" Not exactly what she'd planned to say, then again, she hadn't known what she meant to say anyway.

Wes nodded slowly as if he were afraid if he moved too quickly, he'd scare her off. He wasn't wrong.

"Uh...why don't you come in? It's hot outside." Her words were wooden, her hands shaking as she tried to remember how to be human. She used to be good at this, at knowing how to breathe and think at the same time.

Now, she felt as if she were one bad decision away from falling down the rabbit hole.

She closed the door behind him as he passed her and then turned to face him. His gaze traveled over her, and she knew it wasn't about finding her attractive, but about making sure she was okay. Or at least that's what she felt at that moment.

"You're wet."

Jillian's eyes widened. "Uh."

She swore she saw a blush on his cheeks, and he cleared his throat. "I mean your jeans and shoes. You're tracking water through your house. What's going on?"

She looked down at herself and frowned. "Oh. It's my water heater. The damn thing is going wonky, and I couldn't fix it." She looked up at him and winced. "Uh, that's probably not something I should tell my boss, right?"

Wes sighed. "I'm not your boss right now."

"Firing me, are you?" She knew she sounded on edge, but she was all over the place today.

Wes gave her a look she couldn't interpret. "No, and you know that. I'm saying that, right now, in your home when it's just you and me? I'm not your boss."

"Then what are you, Wes?"

He met her gaze, and she let out a slow breath. "I want to be your friend. I'm tired of fighting all the time. I'm tired of this feeling between us, and I'd rather find a balance. Now, do you want help with your water heater? You're far better at this stuff than I am, but I can hold a wrench for you while you work."

She pressed her lips together, a little stunned that he'd said everything he had. "I...I don't know what we are, Wes. Or what we can be." Emotion clogged her throat, and she tried to push it back just like she had so many times over the past two weeks, but it wasn't as easy as it was before.

"Talk to me, Jilli."

"Don't call me that," she cried out, her hands shaking. Wes took a step toward her, and she held out her trembling hands, knowing her eyes were wide and possibly a little manic.

"Okay, I won't. I'm sorry. I didn't know it bothered you."

And it hadn't every other time he'd called her that, in fact, she'd *liked* it, but right then, she knew she was feeling too much, too soon, and wasn't in control.

"Why did you have to call me in?" she blurted, her voice cracking.

Wes's jaw tightened, and sadness filled his eyes.

"I'll never forgive myself for doing that, for taking those moments away from you."

She moved the two steps toward him and put her palms on his chest, her breath coming in pants.

"I could have helped him. I could have *been there*. Instead, he died alone and without me. I didn't get to say goodbye, Wes. I didn't get to do anything! I left him, thinking I had more time, when all the while, the world was laughing at me because there's never any time. I lost everything, and I'm so fucking mad, Wes. I should have been there. Why did you make me go to the site? Why did that pipe have to burst and ruin everything? Why can't I fix my damn water heater? Why can't I do anything right?"

She didn't let the tears fall, but her heart raced, and her mind went in a thousand different directions.

"Why did he have to die, Wes? Why did he leave me here alone?"

"Oh, fuck," he whispered before he pulled her close and cupped her face with his strong hands. She beat his chest with her fists, so fucking angry at the world, but he didn't back away. He didn't flinch when she hit him harder before resting her palms on the planes of his chest.

"It wasn't your fault," he whispered.

"But he's still not coming back. I should have been there. I should feel *something* beyond this aching cavern of nothingness, yet all I can do is wonder why I'm not numb all the time. Why is that, Wes? Why don't I feel like I should?"

She was whispering now, no longer yelling or hitting or even crying. She just *was*.

"You're feeling like you need to. There's no wrong way to heal, Jillian. Keep hitting me. Yell some more. I can take it."

And he would. He'd do anything to help, yet she knew there was only one thing she needed from him. One thing that was possibly the worst mistake she could make, but she couldn't think of anything else.

"Help me feel again, Wes," she whispered. "Help me feel." She turned her head and leaned into his palm. "I can't...I can't do anything else. Just help me *be*."

He ran his hand through her hair and over her messy ponytail, giving it a tug. "That would be a mistake."

"No, it wouldn't. We are already on this path, and now I want to just be in your arms and forget everything else. I want to forget this pain. Forget what I lost, and what I'll never have. I want to remember what I can be when everything else is out of my mind. Can you do that? Can you help me?"

He let out a shuddering breath as he rested his forehead on hers. "I want you, Jillian. I do, but I don't want to take advantage of you."

"You won't," she said honestly. If anything, she'd be taking advantage of him, but she couldn't stop needing him. Not now.

Wes ran his hand down her back, pulling her closer. "I can't deny that I want you. I'll never deny that. Not again. And if this is what you want? Then I'll be that for you. And tomorrow, I'll be what you need me to be, as well."

What about what he needed, she wondered.

But before she could tell him that or have second thoughts, his mouth was on hers, and she had that spark of sensation that told her that she could *feel* with him.

She arched into him, her body shaking with need as his hands slowly roamed up and down her back. When she bit his lip, needing more, he let out a growl and reached around to grab her ass, lifting her up in the next movement. She wrapped her legs around his waist, pushing into the strong lines of his muscles. She'd known his body held strength, she'd seen it in the way he moved around the site, how he hid it behind those button-down shirts, but feeling it pressed against her turned her on even more.

He turned with her in his arms and walked toward the dining area off the kitchen. She'd have told him to go back to her bedroom, but when he set her on the edge of the table and leaned down to suck her neck, she moaned, not wanting to take another minute away from what they were doing in order to walk to the back of the house.

He just made her feel so damn good, and he made her *forget*.

That was what she needed right now.

No promises. No pain.

Just him.

Wes cupped her face, and she frowned when he stopped kissing her. "Be in the now, Jillian. Come back to me."

She licked her lips before leaning back and pulling off her shirt. She'd been working, so she was wearing a sports bra and not her cleanest or cutest outfit, but she didn't care. She'd be naked soon anyway.

"Jesus," Wes growled. "You're so fucking sexy."

"In a sports bra?" she asked with a laugh.

He cupped her breast over her bra and pinched her nipple through the thin, stretchy cotton material. "It pushes your breasts together, and all I want to do is slide my dick between them and thrust until I come all over your chin. What do you say about that?"

She raised a brow. "Kinky, are we?"

His eyes darkened, and he used his other hand to squeeze her hip. "You don't know the half of it."

If it were possible, she got even wetter. "You'd better show me then, just so I know the rest of it."

"Well, then, I guess I need to take off these work boots of yours and get to work." He winked, and she grimaced. "Though maybe in the future, I'll fuck you with your boots on. It could be kind of sexy."

Future? No, she wouldn't think about that. Not now. Now was for *not* thinking. Later, she'd worry.

"Just not when they're wet like this? If I'm wearing mine, you have to wear yours, too."

"Deal." He kissed her again before stripping off his shirt. She licked her lips, holding out her hand to run her fingers down his skin. His nipples hardened before her eyes, and she leaned forward to lick a tip. "Jesus," he growled. "I need a taste of you."

He slowly skimmed his fingers down her arm, sending shivers along her body, and she sighed, wanting more. Always wanting more, but with Wes, she had a feeling she'd get what she needed—at least for the moments they had together.

In answer to his words, she spread her legs, though she still wore her pants. Wes let out a growl and wrapped his hand around the back of her neck, pulling her close to crush his mouth to hers. She panted with need, craving him more than she thought possible, but before she could get her fill of him, he pulled back and started working on her pants. She helped him with the zipper then gripped the edge of the table and lifted her hips. He slid her pants and panties down in one swift movement, leaving her in only her bra on the long, wooden table.

Wes knelt in front of her, putting his hands on her knees and slowly spreading her before him. "You're already wet," he growled roughly. "I can see you, all glistening and hungry for my cock. Or maybe it's my mouth you want." He traced her outer lips with his finger, and she shuddered, her grip on the table tightening.

Apparently, Wes Montgomery was a dirty talker, and her pussy *really* liked it.

Hell, *she* really liked it.

"If you don't start licking what you're looking at, Wesley, I'm going to have to take matters into my own hands." She licked her lips before sliding one hand down her stomach. She gasped when he gripped her wrist, stopping her.

"Keep your hands on the table. You're going to need it for balance."

Turned on beyond measure, she did as she was told, then let out a long moan as he buried his face between her legs and licked her. Her head lolled back, and she arched her hips, wanting more. His tongue slid in and out of her, teasing. And when she opened her eyes and looked down to see his dark head between her legs, she came on the spot, her body shaking. He sucked on her clit, biting down gently during her orgasm, making her come even harder, then stood up and wiped his short beard.

"You taste fucking amazing."

Head heavy, she blinked and looked down the length of him, wanting to see all of him. "Do I get a taste?"

"Next time," he said, undoing his jeans and stripping down.

Her mouth dropped open when she got a good look at him, the long, lean cords of muscle, the strength in his body. His cock was long and wet at the tip, and she couldn't wait to have it inside her. Nothing she had in the special drawer in her bedroom could ever match up to the glory that was in front of her.

"I like the look on your face," he said with a laugh.

She looked up at him, the break in their movements allowing thoughts of what she was trying to ignore to creep in. She swallowed hard, and he must have seen it on her face because, in the next instant, he was wrapping himself in a condom that he must have had in his wallet and had his hands on her face, kissing her lips, her cheeks, her jaw.

Jillian wrapped herself around him, needing him inside her more than she could say. "Inside me. I need you inside."

"I'm here, Jilli, I'm here." Then he was inside her, stretching her and making her moan. She scooted to the edge of the table, lifting her legs so he could go deeper. And when he moved, she moved with him, their bodies going slow, moving leisurely as he made her come once again, with him following soon after. This wasn't the fast heat she'd thought she needed.

This was something more.

And it scared her.

"Jillian..." Wes rested his head on her forehead. "Don't cry, baby. Don't cry."

She wasn't even aware she'd been crying until he said it, but now that she knew, she cried harder. He was still buried deep inside her, yet he held her close as she sobbed, letting the emotions she'd held at bay for so long finally break.

And Wes held her.

And when she finally woke up from this pain, she'd have to remember that...even if she didn't know what it meant.

CHAPTER THIRTEEN

It had been four days since he was buried inside Jillian and held her when she cried. If she'd been any other woman, he'd have felt weird about having someone cry like that after they made love and he was still *inside* her.

But it had been Jillian, and even though he'd tried not to, he knew her more than he thought he did. She wasn't crying over him, but over everything else weighing heavily on her. He'd just been able to help her let go.

He ran a hand through his hair and sat down on his couch. They'd spoken at work every day since and even texted though it was still a little awkward. They didn't know what they were, and he wasn't sure what, if anything, would happen next, but things had changed.

He snorted and rested his head in his hands. Changed? That was the understatement of the year. They'd been going down this path—whatever road this was—for much longer than the four days he'd been in his head about what had happened.

And the truth was, though he'd been in his head because he was thinking about what would come next, he wasn't feeling weird. Okay, maybe a little weird, but not *that* weird. And considering she used to be with his twin—even in an unconventional relationship he hadn't understood until it was almost too late—it should have felt much weirder than it did.

Now when he thought about Jillian, he thought of *her*. Just Jillian. The woman he'd fought with, kissed, fought with some more, then felt under him, over him, and around him as they'd both come until they could barely catch their breath.

She wasn't Storm's ex anymore.

She was Jillian.

His Jillian? Well, he didn't know about that, and he wasn't sure they would ever find out. So far, they'd done well keeping everything only for that day and not talking about it, but he knew if they *didn't* talk about whether they were going to pursue...whatever this was, it would become that weirdness he dreaded.

Did he want a relationship with Jillian? He honestly didn't know what he wanted. He'd been looking for someone to share his life with, that much he knew, but was Jillian that person? She made him *feel*. That much he knew. In fact, his emotions ran the gambit whenever she was around but was that what he wanted?

"Jesus," he grumbled to himself. In his mind, he was equating a relationship with Jillian to the idea that it would be the forever kind like the rest of his family had. While he didn't want to be left behind when his family settled down, was it fair to him or Jillian to put her in that position? Was that what he wanted?

And maybe once again he was overthinking things.

Okay, there was no maybe about it. Once Wes got stuck in his head, it took a crowbar or lots of alcohol to get him out.

The doorbell rang before he could let those thoughts go down a trail even more twisted. He sighed before pulling himself up off his couch and heading to see who could be at his house during the afternoon. Considering that his family tended to drop by unannounced if they knew he was home, it was probably one of them.

But when he opened the door, it wasn't a family member, it was Jillian with a six-pack of beer in one hand and a brown paper sack in the other. He couldn't help but smile at the sight of her, and that should have told him far more than all the winding thoughts he'd had before she showed up on his doorstep.

"Hey," she said after they'd stood there in silence for a long moment.

"Hey," he said softly.

She cleared her throat. "So, uh, you're probably wondering why I'm here." Before he could answer, she continued. "I brought beer and sandwiches for lunch because I felt weird, and I don't want to feel weird. So, can I come in to just hang out? We don't need to uh...talk or anything, but I felt weird *not* being near you and almost actively avoiding you because of said weirdness."

He laughed and took a step to the side so she could come in. He loved that she was so blunt about it, and he admired her for it. He'd try to be as honest and straight forward with her. He took the beer from her hand and leaned forward, brushing his lips over hers. She sucked in a breath, and he thought he'd fucked up, but then she leaned forward and kissed him back, ever so slightly.

"I'm glad you came by."

Her eyes brightened. "Yeah? Well, now I'm glad I came. I mean...came here. Not came as in what we did on my table."

He snorted and shook his head before taking her hand and leading her to the kitchen. "I'll put the beer in the fridge for later, if that's okay? I didn't sleep much last night, and having a beer right now will just put me to bed."

She winced. "Yeah, I should have brought root beer instead of the hard stuff, but I wasn't thinking. Plus, whenever I need to talk to...uh...other friends and just be, a six-pack and food is sort of my staple."

Wes winced like she had and leaned back against the kitchen counter. "You mean Storm. You bring beer and food when you need to talk with Storm."

Jillian set their lunch down on the counter beside him and leaned back to run her hands over her face. "Yes. He's still my best friend, Wes. And it's weird now. I hate weird."

"It shouldn't be, though. I mean, yeah, it's not exactly easy thinking about you and my brother, but that's in the past." He let out a long breath. "That's in the past. So I think once we get over the awkwardness of bringing him up, we can move on. He's your friend. He's my brother. He's going to be part of our conversations. He works with both of us and isn't going away. Hell, he *shouldn't* go away."

She licked her lips, a frown on her face for a moment, and all he could do was watch that tongue of hers peek out and imagine it on something other than her lips.

"Move on? Are you saying you want to move on with me? With this? Or move on as in not talk about it again."

Wes let out a sigh and moved forward, cupping her face. "I've been thinking about the answer to that

136

question for four days now, and until you walked through that door and made me laugh, I wasn't sure what I was going to say." He leaned forward, brushing his lips against hers again. "I know it's complicated. I know we're probably going to screw up more than once, but I don't want this to end. I want to get to know you like we are now. I want you in my bed. I just want you."

She smiled against his lips and leaned back to meet his gaze. "And, oddly enough, I wasn't sure what my answer would be to that question until I saw you either. I'm in agreement that things are going to get sticky. We also need to tell Storm before things get too serious. Of course, I find having sex to be pretty serious so we might have messed up there."

"Maybe. And while I agree with you that we need to tell Storm because while he might not be part of *this,* he is part of our lives, I don't want to make it too big a deal." He let out a breath. "Because if we make his reaction too important, I feel like we're just setting ourselves up to screw things up."

"And now I'm confused and feeling like it's all too much," she said with a laugh. "We are *so* complicated, even though we keep saying we don't want to make complications."

He ran his fingers down her arms. "Pretty much. So, why don't you tell me what you want, and I'll do the same?"

"You want me to go first?" she asked, clearly not too keen on that idea.

"Like pulling off a Band-Aid right?" he asked with a laugh.

She rolled her eyes. "Yes, because discussing whether or not we're in a relationship should be like an open wound."

They both laughed at that. "Okay, so I'll pull first. I want you, like I said. I want to see where this goes. Yes, we fight, but honestly, I think that kind of turns me on."

"You're a dork." She paused. "But it turns me on, too." A blush stained her cheeks, and he brushed his thumb along the heat of her skin. "And what do I want? Well, the same thing as you, I guess. I don't want to ruin our work relationship. I don't want to hurt our friends. But I want you. I want to see what happens. And I know I'm probably at the worst point in my life to even look at dating anyone, but the thing is, I told myself when I pushed Storm toward Everly that I'd find my own happiness. Or at least try. And after a few too many bad first dates, I want to see what happens with you." She looked up at him, emotion in her eyes. "Does that sound like enough to you."

He trailed his finger over her jaw, his heart pounding. "I think that sounds exactly like what we need. So, let's try it out. See what happens. I want to promise you that I won't hurt you or hurt what you have with Storm, but I can't really. I *can* promise I'll try."

"So..." she said after a moment.

"So..." He cleared his throat. "Why don't we take that beer and lunch and go sit outside on my porch. Then, afterward, I can show you around the property. I'm slowly renovating the barn in the back to be my workshop, but I'm not that far into it yet."

Her eyes brightened. "Need plumbing out there? I know someone who could help."

"Oh, really? I was thinking of someone I know from work, but I hear she's a pain to work with."

He ducked her fist and laughed, bringing her close for a kiss. "Let me show you after we eat."

"I thought you said a beer would make you sleepy," she said, referring to his previous comment.

"I don't think I could be sleepy around you," he whispered. "You rev me up too much."

She grinned. "Oh, Wesley, you say the sweetest things."

"Ever have sex in a barn?" Jillian asked once they'd finish their lunch and were on the end of his tour.

He tripped over his feet and almost landed on his face. "Uh...can't say I have."

She tilted her head. "Interesting."

He laughed and pulled her close. "Is that a proposition?"

She bit his jaw. "Well, it's not like we're in a barn full of cows staring at us."

Wes groaned when she slid her hand between them and squeezed his cock over his jeans. "You'll be the death of me, woman."

"So you say."

He kissed her hard, cupping her ass and pulling her closer to him so her hand was trapped between them. "You know, when I wanted to bring you out here, it was to show you my work, not get into your pants."

"You showed me your etchings, Wesley." She winked before sobering. "I love the place. You're so talented, and I know this workshop is going to kick ass when it's done. But you're not going to take advantage of me by taking me roughly in the barn."

He couldn't help but laugh at the exaggerated way she said the last part of her sentence. "I wanted to take you out on a date before we did this again," he said, rocking into her hold.

"We're doing everything a bit backwards, but I think I'm okay with that. We can have our first date after we have sex again."

He snorted. "Well, maybe our first date was when we got stuck in the elevator. And now our second date was our lunch just now. What do you say?"

"Pretty unconventional, Wesley. I figured you for the convention type."

"Oh, Jilli, if you only knew."

"Well, Wesley, I did just ask you to take me roughly in the barn. So why don't you show me?" She wiggled her hips against him, and he groaned.

"Be careful what you wish for," he growled, biting her jaw.

"Promises, promises." She licked her lips, so he had to kiss her.

Had. To.

He skimmed his hands over her sides, gripping her hips so they rocked together as they stood in his soon-to-be workshop, bodies pressed close as they kissed and explored one another.

"There's one thing I need to do that you wouldn't let me do last time," she said quickly as she pulled away.

"Oh yeah?" he asked.

"Yep. Now, help me take off these pants because if I don't have your dick in my mouth in the next sixty seconds, I'm going to get angry."

He couldn't help but laugh with her as he undid his belt and jeans. She helped him get them off his hips and down to his knees.

"Spread your legs a bit," she ordered as she knelt in front of him, palming his cock through his black boxer briefs. He ran his hand through her hair as he did so and groaned when she sucked on him through the cotton.

"It's not fair that I can't see those pretty tits of yours as you do this."

She grinned up at him and leaned back so she could strip off her shirt. She had her bra off in moments, and he couldn't help but reach down to palm her breasts.

"So fucking sexy," he growled, his calloused finger rubbing along the tip of her nipple. It hardened under his touch, and he pinched, loving the way she groaned. His Jilli liked a little pain with their play, something he'd have to remember.

"Shit, I almost forgot." She stood up quickly and dug into her jeans pocket. Since she was there and he couldn't help himself, he leaned forward and sucked one nipple into his mouth while cupping her other breast in his hand. Jillian let out a moan and leaned into him. "Damn it, Wesley, you're good at that."

He bit down gently before turning his attention to her other breast. "I try."

"Well, stop it, because I wanted to suck your dick and I can't do that with you making me all wet and needy with your mouth on my boobs. Now, here, take this." She handed him a condom, and he smiled. "I'll forget about it if I don't give it to you now. So, if you'll excuse me, I have a dick to suck." And with that, she sank down to her haunches again in only her boots and jeans, pulled his dick from his boxer briefs, and preceded to give him the best blowjob of his life.

He literally saw stars as she sucked on the head, flicking her tongue along the slit. With one hand, she alternately pumped him and cupped his balls while she used her other hand to dig her fingernails into his thigh.

Jesus. Christ.

If he weren't careful, he'd blow his load, and it would all be over too soon. He quickly pulled her away so she stood in front of him, his now wet dick so fucking hard between them he was pretty sure he'd break something if he hit it against anything right then.

"As much as I want to come down your throat, I'm not that young anymore, you know. If I come now, I won't be able to use this condom and fuck you senseless. Your choice. I can still make you come by eating you out, and you know how much I want that. But I was thinking of using that old blanket and draping it over the sawhorse over there and then fucking you from behind while you bend over it. So, you tell me. Fucking you from behind, or eating you after you swallow my come?"

Jillian blinked at him for a moment, and in answer, she quickly undid her pants and was toeing off her boots so fast, she was afraid she'd fall.

"Um...what's your answer, Jilli? My tongue, or my cock. I'll make you feel good either way, but you need to tell me what you want."

She licked her lips as she wiggled out of her panties, and he almost came right then. "The fucking thing. I've never been bent over a sawhorse before, and I'm pretty sure I have wetness running down my thighs right now at the thought, I'm so turned on. Next time, old man, we go for the sixty-nine and feast on each other to our hearts' content. For now, we fuck."

He couldn't help it, he laughed as he stripped off the rest of his clothes. "I love that you're as crass as I am."

She reached for him, gripping him by the cock. "You hide it better in public than I do."

"True. But I like you the way you are." To prove that, he reached between them and cupped her pussy. She was already so wet, she drenched his hand even before he slid two fingers into her very tight, impossibly hot sheath.

"Arguh." He wasn't sure if that was a word or a moan, but he didn't care. He kept his gaze on hers as he pumped his finger in and out of her, having to bend slightly so he could reach her. And as soon as he brushed his thumb over her clit, she came, her cunt tightening around his finger and her body shaking. She gripped his shoulders, and he pumped harder in and out of her, needing her to keep coming on his hand.

"That's it, Jilli. Let's get you past that first edge so I can keep you going longer when I fuck you."

"Pro-mi-ses." Her teeth chattered as she said the word, and he crushed his mouth to hers, needing her lips, her tongue, *her*.

When he pulled away, the two of them practically ran toward the sawhorse, tripping over each other in the process. They put the blanket on top, and he slid the condom over his cock as she bent over in front of him, her ass so firm and round he had to bend over to bite it.

"Hey!" she said, glaring over her shoulder, though she had laughter in her eyes. "Kinky much?"

"You haven't even seen my kinky side." And before she could sputter, he thrust into her to the hilt in one movement. Her eyes practically rolled to the back of her head, and her body shook. He didn't wait for her to calm, instead he pumped in and out of her with such vigor, he was afraid he'd break the sawhorse.

And he didn't give one damn.

He fucked her hard, his cock straining, and his balls tightening. "Use your fingers to make yourself come over my cock, Jilli. Show me how sexy you are. How fucking hot you make me."

She did as she was told and slid her hand over her clit. Two quick brushes later and she was coming around his cock, and he was filling up the condom as they each shouted each other's names.

And before either of them could figure out what they could say after an orgasm like that, someone cleared their throat behind them. Wes and Jillian looked over and froze.

Storm stood there, one hand over his eyes, the other outstretched in front of him. "Uh, I...I didn't know you would be out here. But, uh...keep going. Or maybe you just went from the sound of it. Oh, my God. My eyes. I think they're burning. But...uh...I'm going now. Forget I was here. But, uh...just know that this is cool. I'm good with this. Happy it happened. Well not that I just saw something that will give me nightmares because, dear God Wes, I did *not* need to see your ass like that. Or ever. But I'm happy for the two of you. And now, I'm going. And, well...bye."

Storm scurried away, and Wes was left there, still balls-deep inside of Jillian. The two of them looked at one another and then did the only thing they could do.

They laughed.

"Well, I guess the cat is out of the bag," Wes said as he pulled out of her.

"That was one way to let him know what's going on," Jillian said with a snort. "So...are we okay?" She bit her lip as she waited for his answer.

He leaned forward and kissed her softly. "Yeah, we are. And I think Storm will be too as soon as he gets that image out of his mind."

"We were pretty hot, though, just saying."

He reached forward and pulled her closer. "We were more than hot."

And when they reached for each other again, he knew that they would be okay. As for Storm? Well, they'd talk with his brother soon. From the sound of his twin, though, things might actually be fine between them all.

Wes just hoped that was true because the alternative wasn't something he wanted to think about.

CHAPTER FOURTEEN

Jillian's thighs hurt. Her hips hurt. Her head hurt. *Everything* hurt. But as it was because she'd been thoroughly fucked and hadn't slept because the sex had kept her up all night, she couldn't really complain.

Who knew Wes Montgomery could rock her world four times in one night and she'd still want to go back for more. Only the sun had come up, and the two of them needed to get on with their days.

Still, though, it had been a pretty spectacular way to spend the night.

Of course, now it was the next night, and sadly, she wasn't going to spend it with Wes. They might be going fast in some aspects, but slowly in others. It was the speed that worked for them, and that meant she was going to do her girls' night with her friends like she'd planned and then see Wes at work the next day. They might even try to fit in a date or two.

As for work? Well, she'd promised herself that would *not* get tricky. They'd had a talk about it long into the night, and they decided since Storm already knew what was going on, he and Decker—once he found out—would be in charge of directing Jillian's duties. That way, she didn't have to answer directly to Wes when it came to work matters. Yes, he'd still technically be her boss since he owned the company, but since she worked on many of the sites and not just his, they'd find a way to make it work. The family was so interconnected within the business anyway, it was tough to hold a firm line against personal relationships.

But all of that worry would come later. For now, she would put that aside and enjoy her night with the Montgomery girls. Because of her friendship with Everly and Storm, she'd been invited to a few of these gatherings now, and she enjoyed it. Sometimes, they were held at Taboo; other times, at one of their houses. Today, they were at Autumn's since she was one of the few without children to wrangle, and since they planned on drinking, they weren't going to be at Tabby and Alex's. Alex was going strong through his recovery, but adding temptation within his home was just a jerk move on all accounts.

From what she'd learned since getting to know the Montgomerys, they did their best not to change their routines for Alex since he resented that, but they also tried their best not to make things hard for him. Meaning they had alcohol at family events, but they tried to make sure it wasn't a *thing*. She could only respect and kind of envy the way they worked so well as a family.

"You're lost in thought again," Sierra, Austin's wife said with a laugh. "What's going on over there?" The other woman smiled, her long, almost amber hair glinting in the light. She was strikingly beautiful and always so put together. If Jillian had any sense of style, she'd shop at her boutique, Eden, that was across the street from Taboo and Montgomery Ink. But, alas, that wouldn't ever be the case.

"Uh, nothing, just a long night." Jillian took a long draw from her beer and tried to look innocent. Were her cheeks red? Surely not.

"Hmm," Miranda said with a mock serious expression. "I know that face. That's the I-just-got-laid face. I *like* that face."

Meghan laughed and pulled out her knitting. She was getting really good at it, though Jillian knew she and Adrienne were probably lost causes. "Tell Momma all."

"There's nothing to tell," Jillian lied.

"Ooh," Autumn said as she walked into the room with Tabby, a truly gorgeous man behind them. "What is Jillian lying about?"

Everly leaned into Jillian's shoulder and laughed. "I might know."

Jillian turned to her friend, eyes wide. "No, you don't."

Her friend, Storm's fiancée, just grinned. "I might."

"Okay, you have to tell us," Maya ordered. "But first...hi, Dare, it's nice to see you again."

Jillian shook her head and looked up at the very handsome and rugged man.

"This is my brother, Dare," Tabby explained. "He's here to pester me."

"I have business out here," her brother said, his eyes dancing with laughter.

"You own a bar in Pennsylvania, how is it you have business here?" Tabby asked, tapping her foot.

He bopped her on the nose, and she growled. "Business my little sister doesn't need to know about."

"He's talking about sex," Maya added helpfully. "He has a woman out here. Or a man. Or both." She winked. "Just saying." As Maya had two men, Jillian couldn't help but laugh at the fact that yes, that might actually be true.

"Thank you for that, Maya," he said dryly. "And anyway, hello, ladies. Sorry I'm crashing girls' night, but Tabby and Autumn said I needed to at least stop by since I'm not in town that long."

"Stay!" Miranda said as she stood up. "You can play bartender if you want. We promise not to braid each other's hair and do pillow fights until later."

Jillian couldn't help but laugh as everyone started talking at once. When a group of Montgomerys got together, things got loud, that much she knew, and these were only *some* of them. And considering the huge Montgomery Family Reunion was coming up— something Marie Montgomery had invited her to—she was afraid of the level of noise that would come with that particular event.

Dare gave them all a long look and ran a hand over his beard. She'd never been a beard fan until she met the Montgomerys, and now apparently, she couldn't get enough of them. She loved the way the scruff of Wes's beard—when he had one—felt along her inner thighs, and it was a new thing that any beard reminded her of Wes.

"How about I introduce you to everyone," Tabby said quickly, taking her brother's arm. "You didn't meet everyone the last time you were here. You know, the time when you, Fox, and Loch decided to gang up on Alex to make sure I was being treated right?"

Jillian smiled with the others but didn't laugh. Who would confront Wes for her? Storm? No, that wasn't quite the same, was it. She didn't have anyone left to make sure she was being treated right. She ran a hand over her chest, that familiar ache no less heavy than before but at least she was getting used to it.

"So, this is Sierra, Austin's wife. He's the one that owns Montgomery Ink with Maya, Alex's sister." Tabby pointed over at the very inked and pierced woman who sat on the floor by the coffee table. "Maya's married to Jake and Border, but I don't think you met them. Next to Maya is Miranda, another of Alex's sisters. She's married to Decker, who works at Montgomery Inc. with me. Then there's Meghan, the last sister, who also happens to work at Montgomery Inc. and is married to Luc, yet another coworker." Tabby laughed as Dare's eyes widened at all the information. "Since we're talking about the construction company, Jillian over there works with us, as well as Everly's fiancé, Storm. Storm is also a Montgomery, as is his twin, who also works with me." She let out an exaggerated breath, and everyone laughed. "Then there's Autumn, who is amazing and works for Montgomery Ink—the tattoo shop— sometimes. She's also married to Griffin, the last Montgomery brother. And thank God you're leaving before the reunion next week, or I'd have to introduce you to forty other family members that I don't actually know."

Dare was silent for so long that Jillian was afraid they'd broken him. Finally, he cleared his throat. "Uh, hello. I'm Dare. Which you know. From now on, I will be calling you letters of the alphabet, which will change each time I see you because, dear God, Tabby, I don't know if you could have been any more confusing. Aren't you the organized one?"

Tabby stuck out her tongue, and he pinched her cheek. Such a big brother thing to do—not that Jillian knew that personally since she didn't have any family left.

She took another sip of her beer, annoyed that her thoughts were so off tonight. Yes, she was mourning, but she didn't have to wallow over something she'd never have.

"As for being your bartender," Dare continued. "I can do that for a bit. I never get to see Tabs anymore since she moved out to this boondock state."

"Excuse me? I live in *Denver*. You live in our tiny hometown that still thinks prohibition is a thing."

The two argued as they followed Autumn to the kitchen, leaving the others to laugh uncontrollably. It felt good to laugh, to feel free when she was anything but.

Once Dare returned with a batch of margaritas and a special drink that he refused to reveal the ingredients of, but which Jillian knew would be too much for her since she was driving, he said his goodbyes, leaving the girls to joke around and, of course, talk about men.

Jillian went to set her beer down on the side table and frowned when she saw a pair of reading glasses wedged between the couch cushions. She dug for them and looked at the lenses to see if they were salvageable and blinked when she noticed that they were just glass and not prescription.

"Uh, I found some costume glasses in the couch," Jillian said as she passed them over to Autumn. "Are they real? Or are they those blue tinted ones people use for screens."

For some reason, that question made the redhead blush. "Uh...well..."

"Oh my God," Maya said on a laugh. "You wear them for sex games with Griffin, don't you? I mean, you are his personal assistant sometimes, right?"

"Oh! So you do *dic*tation?" Tabby said with an exaggerated eyebrow wiggle.

Autumn was, if possible, even redder.

Maya covered her eyes with her hands and groaned. "Why did I put that image into my head?"

Meghan's knitting needles clinked together loudly as she snorted. "Maya, honey, you have sex with not one, but two men in every room of your house and you're worried about images in your head? Please."

That set everyone off, and then somehow, they were all sharing the oddest places they'd had sex. The fact that three of the women were sisters and the other women were married to the Montgomery brothers only made it that much funnier since Maya, Meghan, and Miranda kept trying to close their eyes and ears at some parts.

"So, Jillian, tell us the best place you've had sex," Autumn said, wearing her glasses and making everyone laugh.

Everly reached out and patted Jillian's arm. "If it was with Storm, that's fine. I know my man is pretty great in the sack."

Wes was better.

Not that she'd say that but...

"From behind on a sawhorse," she blurted. "Best. Ever."

"You and Storm had sex on a sawhorse?" Tabby asked, eyes wide.

Everly's eyes danced with laughter, and Jillian buried her face in her hands. "That wasn't Storm, was it, Jillian Reid? That was the man you're not telling us about." She clucked her tongue, and Jillian was pretty sure she was going to have to strangle her friend.

"Tell us!" Miranda exclaimed, the others joining in on a chant.

"Fine." Jillian threw up her hands. "Fine. It was Wes. Wes freaking Montgomery. That Wes. Storm's twin. He rocked my world and made me almost pass out from coming. Best sex ever, and I'm pretty sure we're going to try to top it the next time we see each other."

Everyone was silent for a moment before Maya raised her arm in victory. "I knew it! Told you! All of you. You doubt my radar, but I can see sex vibes a mile away."

"Says the woman who took a decade to realize she was in love with her best friend, but whatever," Meghan murmured, still knitting away and not even looking up as she spoke.

"Ditto," Maya shot back, and the girls laughed again.

"I'm so happy for you," Everly whispered as the others started peppering her with questions that Jillian wasn't sure she had the answers for.

"It's not too strange?"

"Never," Everly said quickly, her voice sure. "It's what you need it to be, and we support you."

"Damn straight," Maya put in.

She smiled, relaxing once again when the others didn't once make her feel like she was being judged. These people were honestly too good to be true, but she wasn't going to hide from them and their comfort any longer.

They ate pizza, and most of them drank more than they normally would have. Jillian just laughed with them. A lot of them did not have to work the next day since it was a holiday, but since they usually had to be up early for their kids, having a night like this wasn't exactly common.

She said her goodbyes when she was ready to head home and texted Wes like she'd promised, telling him she was on her way. Most of the husbands had come by to pick up anyone who had been dropped off so they could have more than the one beer she had, but since the others hadn't known about Wes until tonight, she'd declined his offer of having him drive her there and back.

By the time she got home, she was exhausted and ready to crawl into bed. The others might not have a workday in the morning, but she had to visit the warehouse site to at least check on things before taking the afternoon off. While Storm and the others had told her it could wait until Tuesday, she didn't feel comfortable doing that after the large leak.

She had her phone out to text Wes that she'd made it home, something that made her feel oddly giddy inside when she paused. Something felt...off. She looked around the house, her senses on alert. Nothing seemed out of place, but she could have sworn it felt as if someone had been in her house. She didn't know why, but it was like everything was just slightly off-kilter.

Phone in hand, she searched the house, but didn't find anything and frowned. Nothing was wrong. She'd just had a long night and a longer day, and she was losing it.

She sent the text to Wes and put all thoughts of strangers being in her house out of her mind. There was no reason anyone would be in her place, and no one had a key, so she was just going crazy. A weird feeling did not equal proof.

Jillian fell asleep face down on her bed, shoes still on, even as she told herself she had nothing to worry about.

Because she didn't.

Right?

CHAPTER FIFTEEN

Wes took a deep breath and tried not to panic, but he couldn't really help the tightening in his chest at the sound of all of them. At last count, there were forty-nine, maybe *fifty* Montgomerys around his parents' home and backyard. Somehow, his formerly expansive childhood home was filled to the brim with family members that he either saw almost daily or for only events like this.

How had his mother and father arranged all of this without help from their children?

How the hell was he going to remember all of his cousins' names without looking at his tablet?

The funny thing was, he *knew* these people, knew their names and faces, yet with all of them together in one place, it was overwhelming. He didn't even want to think about what some of the newer additions to the family would think.

Or Jillian.

Hell, he couldn't believe his mother had invited her, but then again, he would be glad to have her as a lifeline once she finally got there. Because he had a feeling with this many people in one area and with the shared and tangled histories they had, things could get interesting.

Or they'd be completely boring, and everyone would go home and wonder why they didn't do this more often.

You never could tell what you were getting yourself into with a Montgomery function.

"So, you ready to head out there?" Storm asked as he came to Wes's side.

Wes hadn't exactly been hiding from anyone since, hell, he'd worked with his family all week at the site—and Jillian for that matter—but they hadn't actually spoken about the barn incident and what it all meant.

"Mom will find us when it's time," Wes hedged.

Storm shook his head and laughed. "True enough." There was an awkward pause, and Wes really wished he had a beer or soda in his hand. Anything so he could keep busy instead of feeling uncomfortable next to his twin.

"So...you and Jillian?" Storm didn't sound angry or frustrated, just curious. And despite the fact that Storm hadn't punched him in the barn or at work, Wes was still a little worried that his brother would snap and get pissed off.

"Yep." He swallowed hard. "I know we probably should have talked to you first but..."

"Hell no, you shouldn't have talked to me first. You're my brother, and she's my friend. My best friend at that. And though she and I have history, it's not something that is going to stand in the way of her happiness. She never once stood in the way of mine and Everly's. If you make each other happy, I would be a bastard for griping about the fact that you're

together. I'm sure at some point I'll give each of you
the speech about if you hurt her or if she hurts you I'll
kick some ass, but other than that, it's not my
business." He paused, and this time, it wasn't
awkward. "I'm happy for you, though. Jillian's a good
woman and deserves a good man. And, Wes? You're
the best man I know."

And now Wes was *this* close to crying in the
middle of his parents' house. "You're a fucking rock
star. Just saying."

Storm smiled wide. "Yeah, I am. Everly tells me so
every night."

Wes flipped his brother off, grateful that the kids
were outside playing. His phone buzzed, and he
looked down to see a text from Jillian telling him
she'd parked down the street. With so many cars, he
was surprised she'd found any parking at all.

"Jillian's here. I'm going to get her and then meet
you guys out there."

"Sounds like a plan," Storm said, his gaze on the
windows that faced the yard. "Come find me when you
can, we'll hide from the cousins if we need to." He
winked and strode off, leaving Wes laughing.

Wes made his way outside and met Jillian as she
was walking toward the house. "Hey, you," he
whispered, kissing her softly, knowing they were alone
for the time being. He wasn't sure if she wanted to be
here as his...girlfriend, woman, significant other...or
here only because of his mother's request. He'd let
Jillian decide since she was the newcomer in this
situation.

She licked her lips, and he held back a groan.

He'd missed her, damn it. Their one stolen night
during the week hadn't been enough. Yeah, he was
falling fast for her, but damn it, he couldn't help it.

"So, are there like forty bearded dudes in there with some inked women sprinkled throughout?" Jillian asked, her eyes bright.

Wes shook his head, a smile playing on his face. "Some of the cousins shaved, and Griffin just shaved off his beard since he finished his book and likes to feel human. His words, not mine. As for the ink? Well, some of it is showing from what I could tell, but I know that every single cousin either has or will get the Montgomery iris. You know, the MI in the middle of a circle with the flowers on the side? Mom and Dad designed it as a logo for the company years ago, and it sort of transferred over to most of the other companies and then became a family logo. The cousins picked it up, and now it's sort of a thing. I have a feeling Austin and Sierra's boy, Leif, is going to be the first of the next generation to get theirs done. His dad is a tattoo artist, after all, and he's the oldest little one."

Jillian ran her hand over his shoulder and winked. "Well, as I've licked over your tattoo, I do have to say, it's a good design."

He shook his head, smiling as he kissed the top of her head. His Montgomery logo was buried in a broken wall surrounded by a dragon on his shoulder blade. The dragon went down his back but wasn't too big in the grand scheme of things. Austin and Maya had worked on it together since he didn't have as much ink as the rest of his family and having them take turns was the only way to appease them.

"Let's go inside, Wesley. I'm not late, as your mother told me to be here at this time, but I'm not about to *be* late because you're trying to neck with me outside."

"Neck? How old are you?" He winked and then let out an *oof* as she punched him in the gut. She didn't hit as hard as she could have since she was still playing, but damn.

"Lead the way, Montgomery."

"You can't call me that in there. Fifty people will turn their heads."

The grip on his hand tightened, and he soothed her knuckles with his thumb. "That's a whole lot of Montgomerys."

"Gird your loins," he whispered, and she threw her head back and laughed.

That was the first glimpse his parents got of her when they walked through the door—Wes grinning like a fool, and Jillian laughing, leaning into him at his words. And while he might have been slightly worried what his parents would think about him and Jillian, he knew he shouldn't have been.

"You're here!" his mom said as she walked toward them, arms outstretched. "I'm sorry I haven't been by since we last saw each other, but planning this thing got a little crazy."

Wes rocked back on his heels as he watched Jillian hold his mother back just as tightly. He knew she was still feeling lost after losing her father and that his parents helped her during the funeral and wake, so he was happy that she could have them now to lean on if needed. She was already so connected to his family, and they'd just started dating. He probably should have been worried about that, but he couldn't make himself be. Everything just felt...good.

And after so many years of feeling left behind and then not so good with Jillian when they'd first met, he'd take this reaction any day.

Jillian said something he couldn't catch and then stood straight as his mother patted her on the cheek. "Thank you for having me. Really. Though from the noise from outside, it sounds like you have a full army out there."

"One or two," his mother said with a wink. "Now hold onto Wes and make some introductions. He'll make sure you don't stray into a field of Montgomerys, never to be heard from again.

Wes held out his hand and laughed as Jillian's eyes widened before she clung comically to his side. "There, there. The Montgomerys don't bite."

His dad laughed a little too hard. "If that's what you think, Wes, you're not living up to your full Montgomery potential."

"And on that note..." He tugged Jillian closer and led her to the French doors at the back of the house. "Ready?"

"As ready as I'll ever be."

Again, he laughed and opened the doors. The sound was almost deafening, and there were so many people at once who looked like family members—dark hair, light eyes, and ink—he was afraid he'd fumble all the introductions.

"So. Many. Beards." He barely heard Jillian's whisper beneath the cacophony of sound, but he still chuckled.

"Let's do this." He nodded to one group in a corner. "Okay, that's half of the Denver Montgomerys. You know them."

She nodded and leaned into him so they could talk easier over the din. "Yes, Wesley. I know who Storm and Everly are. Thanks for that."

"Just checking, Jilli. Let me introduce you to one of the smaller groups." He led her to one of the tables his parents had set up and waved.

"Shep, good to see you, man."

His cousin smiled, his eyes crinkling just a little at the corners. Considering how much this particular cousin had to smile about these days with his wife and child at his side, Wes figured he'd be getting more of those lines soon.

"Hey, Wes, have you met Livvy?" He gestured toward the toddler in Shep's wife's arms. "Looks just like Shea, right?"

"Not yet." Wes winked, and the little girl ducked her head behind her mom's neck. Shy. But considering she was a Montgomery, that might not last long.

"She's adorable," Jillian said softly.

"Guys, this is Jillian. Jillian, these are the Colorado Springs Montgomerys. Or rather, they're mostly from there since Shep now lives in New Orleans."

"Not for long," Shep corrected.

Wes's eyes widened. "What?"

"Things are changing," Adrienne, the eldest girl of this particular branch put in. "Lots of good things we can talk about later." She came forward and hugged Jillian hard. "Hey, girl. Did you finish your scarf?"

Jillian shook her head. "I don't think I'll ever cut it as a knitter."

Adrienne nodded, the laughter in her eyes mixed with sympathy. They all knew who that scarf had been for. "I think Meghan might be the only knitter."

"Maybe I'll try it out," Thea put it softly. "Hi, by the way. I'm Thea. Since Wes introduced us as 'the guys.'" She rolled her eyes as she said it and held out her hand. Jillian took it, and then Wes reached around to tug her close. She squealed when he ran his knuckles over her hair. "Stop that right now, Wes Montgomery."

"This is why I call him Wesley," Jillian said as she tugged Thea away. "He just does Wesley things."

Wes let out a groan. Great. Now the whole family was going to call him that.

Roxie's eyes narrowed as she studied him. "Wesley, huh? I like it. I'm Roxie. Nice to meet you."

"She's the baby of the family," Shep said.

Roxie waited until little Livvy was turned the other way before flipping her brother off. "I'm not the youngest cousin. One of those guys takes that title." She waved over at the large groupings of people.

"Has Wes introduced you to everyone?" Adrienne asked.

"Not yet, but I know that no matter what happens, I'll never remember their names." Jillian turned an apologetic glance at Roxie and Thea. "I will forget your names in about ten minutes but never forget your faces. I just happened to have met Adrienne a couple of times before so I'll remember that. Sorry."

Thea waved her off, and Roxie laughed. "It's really okay. We Montgomerys tend to multiply."

Roxie nodded. "And we've had our whole lives to memorize the family tree. I'm pretty sure you'll be able to decline the quiz that will be offered at the end of the party."

"Quiz?" Jillian asked.

"Oh, you know," Wes said offhandedly. "Who is who, who is married to whom, which child is which, what jobs do they have now, who is next in line to get married. All the good stuff."

Jillian's eyes widened. "I...I have no idea how your family is so big. I only had my dad for so long and..." She trailed off, and he held her to his side, kissing the top of her head.

"Well, you're a Montgomery now," Shea said. "I married in, of course, but marriage isn't the only way to be part of the family. Once you're part of the circle, you're kind of assimilated."

"One of us. One of us."

The fact that Adrienne, Roxie, and Thea chanted at the same time only made it that much funnier.

"Okay, so, who is who?" Jillian asked, turning to face the other groups.

He pointed at one group. "Those four are the Montgomerys that now live in Boulder." He gestured to each one and told her their names, though he knew she'd never remember them. "The others that you don't recognize are the five from Fort Collins. Some of them brought dates, and I can honestly tell you I don't remember if anyone is married or not." He winced. "My brain hurts."

Jillian rubbed her temple. "Don't talk to me about your brain hurting when you've met these people before."

"Yes, but never all at once. I mean, not since we were little kids. Anyway, that's all of us. Now, I need food and a beer because that was exhausting."

Jillian lifted on her toes and kissed his jaw. "A beer sounds pretty good, Wesley."

He growled and narrowed his eyes. "I'm not going to forget that you told the others what you call me."

She shrugged. "True, but you'll only like it when I call you that, won't you? I see the way your eyes darken and the fact that your breath catches just a bit when I say it. You *like* it."

"I like you." He shrugged when her eyes widened. "Just saying." He reached around and spanked her softly, even with all of his family watching. He'd apparently gone crazy. "Food, woman. And a beer. Let's go."

"Onward, noble steed," she said as she moved to the side.

He laughed, holding her close as they walked, aware the others were watching them, and for some reason, he truly didn't care. He didn't know how it had happened, but he'd fallen for Jillian Reid.

What he was going to do about it? He didn't know, but the idea that he was comfortable enough to be himself with her with so many of his family members looking on and wondering, well, that meant something.

And when they were alone, he'd do his best to figure out what exactly what that something was.

CHAPTER SIXTEEN

This wasn't going to be weird. There was no way tonight would be weird. And if Jillian kept repeating that to herself, she might believe it. Her stomach rolled, and she let out a breath. After everything that had happened recently in her life, a double date with her boyfriend, his twin—who happened to be her best friend and ex-friends with benefits—and that man's fiancée, who also happened to be Jillian's new friend shouldn't be that big of a deal.

And considering how many words it took to describe the four of them, no wonder her brain hurt.

Wes reached over and gripped her hand even as he kept his attention on the road in front of them. "You're going to give me a panic attack if you don't calm down."

She glared at him and hoped he could see her out of the corner of his eye. "You say that, and yet you look remarkably calm."

He gave her a squeeze before taking his hand back so he could make the turn into the parking lot. "It's just my brother and his fiancée. We just had a huge reunion where you met a million and one Montgomerys, yet right now, you look more freaked than you did then."

He turned to her after he'd parked and shut off the engine, and she couldn't help but calm ever so slightly when he looked at her. Perhaps *calm* wasn't quite the right word since he revved her personal engine every time he was near her and had before she even realized what that chemistry was. Nothing about Wes Montgomery calmed her, but having him next to her like this helped her find her breath just a little bit easier.

"It's just bar food and pool, nothing too scary or fancy," Wes said as he traced her jawline with his finger. She swallowed hard at the sensation of his calloused touch on her skin, annoyed with herself for getting hot and bothered before this doomed double date.

"So you say..." She shook her head and let out a breath. She was making something out of nothing and needed to just take a step back and live in the moment. Wasn't that what she'd been telling herself recently about her and Wes? If she kept stressing out, she wouldn't be the same woman she thought she was, and she wasn't sure if she liked that idea. In fact, she didn't like it at all.

"Let's go in and get a beer. It'll help with the nerves."

"How can you not be freaking out just a tiny bit?" she asked as she leapt out of the truck.

"Because I told myself I was going to be okay tonight." He shrugged as he took her hand, and the two of them made their way into the bar. "And I'll probably freak out later. It's how I roll."

She couldn't help but laugh, and the two of them cracking up was probably the first sight Storm and Everly had of them when they walked in. Everly beamed at them, and Storm, for some reason, looked relieved. Apparently, Jillian wasn't the only one slightly on edge about tonight.

"I'm glad we weren't late," Everly said as she hugged them both. "The boys were being a little clingy as we left them with the sitter."

Jillian winced. "I'm sorry for taking you away from them." She knew the twins had been dealing with health problems all their lives, and it couldn't be easy for Everly to leave them with another caretaker.

"You're not taking me away from them," Everly said with a smile. "Every once in awhile, Storm and I need adult time, and the boys really do love hanging out with their grandparents and the sitter. They were just a little clingy tonight, but they probably already forgot about it with the promise of board games and sugar." She shrugged. "It's sort of the babysitter way."

"Anytime you need to leave, though, just tell us."

"Feeling nervous?" Everly asked as the men went to get drinks.

"Just a little." The two women claimed a pool table, and Jillian shooed away two other guys who came over to either play with them or put the moves on. She glared at another guy who sidled right up to them, and Everly snorted as the man skittered away.

"Why is it that two seemingly single women can't enjoy a game of pool without dudes coming over to 'help'?" Everly asked as she chalked her cue.

"Because us little ladies could only be in here to have a big man help us with our sticks...or would it be their sticks?"

"Whose sticks?" Wes asked as he set a pitcher of beer down on the table nearest them, and Storm followed with the cups. Since they were plastic, Jillian figured that's why Storm carried them and not the large pitcher. Between the three of them, no one would be letting Storm lift anything too heavy for a long while yet.

Wes wrapped an arm around Jillian's waist and pulled her close, so she leaned into him. As Everly did the same to Storm, it didn't seem as awkward. For some reason, seeing Everly so at ease with the situation made it easier for Jillian to enjoy herself. Maybe if she got out of her head, she'd be able to just go with the flow.

"Just dudes," Jillian finally answered. "No one special." She wiggled her ass slightly over his crotch since she could feel him against her, and he stiffened in more ways than one. Poor guy.

"Well, just let us know if we need to kick some ass," Storm said as he kissed the top of Everly's head.

"I'm pretty sure we can handle that ourselves," Jillian drawled. "Considering playing pool is my thing, as is getting guys to keep their sticks away from my cue."

Wes growled, and she hip-checked him before moving toward Everly, adding a slight sway to her hips. This was getting fun.

"Girls against boys?" Everly asked, clearly enjoying her self, as well. She wrapped her arm around Jillian's waist, and Jillian batted her eyelashes at Wes.

The two men glanced at one another and shook their heads, grins on their faces. "You know," Storm began, "people used to think that Wes and I shared women. Like we'd end up with one wife between us or some shit like that."

Jillian snorted, and Everly just sighed. Storm had said it low enough that no one would hear, but still, they were in public.

"Not gonna happen, buddy," Jillian said, pointing her cue at them both.

Wes held up his hands in surrender. "God, no. No freaking way. And I have no idea why my dear brother even brought that up." He narrowed his eyes at Storm, and Jillian and Everly laughed.

"I'm just saying, with the way the two of you are cozying up to each other, I figured I'd let you know."

Jillian flipped him off and laughed. "Whatever, dude. Now let's play some pool, and we'll kick your ass *without* making out like the guys behind you want us to do."

Wes glared over his shoulder, and the two big dudes walked away as if they hadn't been eyeing Jillian and Everly. Pool halls and bars were oftentimes a blast; other times, she preferred to be home. Sure, she was the better pool player of the four of them and played with some of the guys at the bar closer to her house occasionally, but for tonight, she would just have fun on this double date, drink a beer, and eat yummy nachos with extra cheese.

And if she had a little fun by flirting with Wes *and* Everly at the same time? Well, that just made it better and easier.

"So..." Jillian whispered into Wes's ear. "What do you want to wager?" She bit his earlobe, and he growled again.

"What are you offering?" His hand went to her ass, and she could feel the slight buzz of her single beer flowing through her system.

She kissed his jaw and winked. "Whoever loses has to make the other person come with their mouth as soon as we get back to your place."

He let out a groan, and she bit her lip to keep from joining him. Everly and Storm were in the middle of a conversation that seemed just as heated, and she was glad no one could overhear either of the couples.

"Deal. Better get those knee pads out, baby, because I'm thinking you're going to need them when you suck me off tonight."

She rolled her eyes and moved away from him, brushing her fingers over his cock ever so slightly. "You wish, Montgomery."

"Hell yeah, I do."

She snorted and went to Everly's side. Either way, she'd win tonight because while she loved giving Wes blowjobs, the idea of his head between her legs as he sucked her clit made her dampen her panties.

It would be a long night, and she couldn't wait to get home.

And with the way Wes kept his eyes on her curves, she had a feeling he felt the same way.

By the time they'd made it back to Wes's place, she was so damn horny she wasn't sure she could even make it inside the door. They'd said goodbye to Storm and Everly and had practically run to Wes's truck. Since the other couple had done pretty much the same thing to Storm's vehicle, Jillian had a feeling she and Wes weren't the only two on edge.

Wes closed the door behind her and somehow tackled her to the ground without hurting either of them. She let out a grunt, and Wes started sucking on her neck.

"You win," Wes growled. "Now, let's get these pants off because I need to have your pussy on my face. Now."

"That's what I like to hear," she said on a strained laugh. Together, they undid the button of her jeans and slid the zipper down. She lifted her hips to help him pull off the tight denim, leaving her in just her panties and top since she'd tossed off her flip-flops as soon as they walked into the house.

Before she could say another word, Wes had his mouth over her panties and was kissing her pussy, his warm breath and touch sending her over the edge embarrassingly quick.

"That's it. Come on my face." He pulled her underwear aside and licked her, sucking on her clit and nibbling on her lower lips even as he speared her with three fingers at once. He stretched her quickly, sending a shocked gasp from her lips before she came a second time in as many minutes.

Before Wes, she hadn't thought that was even possible.

He draped her legs over his shoulders and continued to eat her out, drawing every moan and gasp from her that he possibly could as he explored her cunt with his mouth. And when she came *again*, she tugged on his hair for mercy.

"I can't do it again, I need..."

He grinned before kissing her hard and jumping to his feet. He quickly stripped out of his clothes and reached down to pull her up to her feet. His cock was hard between them, slapping his belly as he moved.

"Bathroom," he growled out, and she blinked.

"Huh?"

"I'm not going to last long, and I had this idea about shower sex earlier that I can't get out of my head." He slapped her bare ass, and she groaned. Only he could get away with that, and only in private. "Come on. I want to fuck you in the shower."

She licked her lips as she looked down at his *very* thick cock. "Well, come on then." She turned on her heel and stripped out of the rest of her clothes as she ran toward the bathroom. They both laughed as they left a pile of clothes in their wakes, touching and caressing as they played around, waiting for the water to heat.

Then he had a condom on, and the two of them were in the shower. He set her on the slight edge that rose from the side and slid into her in one thrust. Water slicked down them, making it hard to hold on, but she tightened her grip *and* her pussy so she wouldn't lose him.

That made him groan, and he leaned down to suck her nipple into his mouth, even as he thrust. They both clung to one another, their breaths coming in pants as they fucked hard in the shower.

And before she could fully lose herself in this man, she was coming again, Wes's shout ringing in her ears, telling her that he was coming right along with her.

She held onto him, her body shaking in the cooling water, and Wes's body doing the same.

This was what she'd been missing all those times she thought to hide from any kind of forever.

This.

What she would do about it, however, she didn't know.

CHAPTER SEVENTEEN

Wes groaned and rubbed the back of his neck. He might be healed from his attack in the alley, but he wasn't as young as he used to be. He'd spent the past week dealing with problem after problem on this warehouse job, and he was just about ready to throw in the towel for the day. He'd known the building wouldn't be easy, and the fact that it had been abandoned and out of use for so many years only added to that, but if he were a superstitious man, he'd have called this project cursed.

Pipes burst on a whim before Jillian even had a chance to start on that side of the building. Subfloors that had looked decent enough at the start were now too weak to hold up new flooring. Windows shattered or had rocks thrown through them from vandals after years of not being touched before this. Their security teams hadn't been able to catch anyone, and that just pissed off everyone at Montgomery Inc. even more.

He was just freaking exhausted and needed a weekend to start over and get his head back in the game. Added into all of that was the fact that he hadn't been able to see Jillian since their double date. They'd texted and even tried a little phone sex the night before, but it wasn't enough. He'd quickly become addicted to her, and he hadn't meant to.

She'd been on the other four project sites for the company all week with her newly hired cohorts helping at the warehouse while she finished up the main plumbing projects on the bookstore and other places. Once she cleared those from her plate, she could work at the warehouse full-time again, but this week just hadn't worked out timing wise. Of course, that meant they'd have to also ensure that they were handling this new way of working together the right way. Storm, Tabby, and Decker had all agreed to deal with any work issues that came up between Wes and Jillian for now, but it would be a little different when they worked together next week.

When he'd voiced his concerns, she'd only sighed at him before saying, "You know what? I already deal with bullshit from guys who think they know better than me because I'm a woman. This particular company is better than most, but even you can't take away everyone's ingrained concepts of what women and men can do. As long as *we* don't put ourselves in a bad situation where we don't trust each other, then we'll be fine. The family is *so* connected and overlapping that I know the men and women on the sites day in and day out aren't really going to blink an eye anymore once they find out that we're dating. And if they do? Fuck 'em."

"That's my girl," he'd said before he proceeded to ask her what she was wearing, making her laugh before making her moan.

And even though the thought of what they'd said to each other that night warmed him, he was honestly so exhausted that he didn't know if he had the energy for anything other than sitting around in his underwear with an ice-cold beer that night.

"You heading home?" Storm asked as he walked up to Wes's side. While Storm normally spent his time either in the office or at the bookstore these days, with so many setbacks on the warehouse, his brother had come out to alter some of the designs as they got to know the building better and figured out what would work and what wouldn't. He'd be in and out even more once they were actually able to split up the building like they wanted to for each of the small businesses. They were going to get to that in the next week, thank God. They were already behind, and that was not somewhere Wes liked to be. But like he'd thought before, the place felt as though it were cursed.

"Yeah," Wes said after a moment, taking the bottle of water Storm held out to him. "This has been just one of those weeks, you know?"

Storm nodded, drinking some of his own. His twin might not be lifting or doing any of the physical work since Wes would kick his ass if he tried while he was still healing, but it was still damn hot.

"It's looking good, but it's the biggest job we've ever taken on, by far. All I want is a nap after playing with the boys and cuddling with Everly. You know?"

Wes couldn't help but smile at that idea. "Yeah, I know."

"But with Jillian, right?" Storm winked. "I like the way you are around each other now. I mean, back when Jillian and I were, well, whatever we were, I was afraid you'd both kill each other rather than do what you're doing now. Either you were both hiding your feelings, or you realized you were different than who you thought you were."

Wes snorted. "That was confusing, but I get it. Jillian and I had incorrect preconceived notions of each other." He paused, wondering if he should say anything but deciding to anyway. The rest of the crew was already on their way out of the building, leaving the two of them alone. "Why didn't you punch me? Or ask me to state my intentions initially?"

Storm stuffed his hands into his pockets and rocked back on his heels. "I thought we got our fighting out of our system before."

Wes grunted. The two of them had punched and wrestled, letting years of unsaid resentment and secrets bubble to the surface. "I guess we might have."

Storm let out a breath. "I'm not going to use my fists for her decisions. And if you're both happy? Then I'm happy. And you know what? I felt like shit when I realized we'd used each other as crutches for so long. So the fact that she's moving on and finding what she needs means everything. It helps that she and Everly are so close now, too, you know?"

Wes nudged his shoulder against Storm's. "I guess we're lucky our family is so close."

"True. We've been through hell the past few years with everything going on. It's nice to be able to just *be*. And speaking of, I promised Everly I'd be home on time for dinner. You have plans with Jillian?"

Wes shook his head. "Tomorrow. Tonight, I'm going to lounge in my underwear like God intended."

Storm laughed, and the two of them headed out to their trucks after checking in with security. They were still on alert after everything that had happened to the site, and Wes hated the extra expense, but he hoped to hell it was worth it.

By the time he got home, the air conditioning in his truck had only just begun to cool him down. He shuffled inside, and since he wasn't a heathen, walked all the way to the back of the house where his master bedroom was before he stripped down to his boxers.

Then since he was already there, he got completely naked, stuffed his clothes into the hamper, and took a quick shower to get the top layer of grime and dirt off his skin. Feeling better already, he put on a pair of gym shorts without bothering to put on boxers again and strode out to his kitchen. As soon as he pulled a beer from his fridge, he opened it and took a long pull. He'd get something for dinner later, either ordering in or picking out something from his freezer. But for now, he decided to do what he'd told Storm he'd do and sat on his couch drinking a beer.

It had been such a hard week, yet he knew they were accomplishing something far greater than themselves. He just had to remember that when his body ached and his head pounded.

He was just about to settle into mindless TV and call Jillian when his phone rang. Sadly, it wasn't the woman he wanted to talk to.

"We got a problem, boss," Frances, the head of his security team at the warehouse said as soon as he answered. She was damn good at her job and had helped them in the past, but there was just something off about this damn place. She and her team had been hired by his brother-in-law Border's company in fact.

"What is it?"

"The motion lights and alarm were tripped, but no one, *no one* got past us. Not sure what's going on, but we called the cops. They're here already, and they don't need you to come down since they can't see anything off, but they're going to want to talk to you."

"Damn it," he growled into the phone, leaning forward to pinch the bridge of his nose.

He talked to the police once Frances put them on, and he went over what had been happening over the past few weeks. Despite that, he got nothing out of it. The police thought it was probably just kids trying to

dare each other or some shit, but Wes was beyond
tired of it. After he'd hung up, he wanted nothing
more than to just go to bed and ignore his day, but of
course, the doorbell rang.

Growling, he set down his phone and stomped to
the front door, only to freeze on the spot when he
opened it. Jillian stood on his porch wearing a trench
coat and very, *very* sexy fuck-me pumps on one of the
hottest days of the year.

"Gonna let me in, Wesley, or should I put on a
show out here?"

He swallowed hard. "A show?" he asked, even as
he moved to the side so she could strut her way inside.
And damn did she strut.

She turned on her heel and didn't wobble a bit. He
was pretty sure his cock had tented his shorts to the
point it was embarrassing, but he didn't give a damn.
He'd never been so turned on, and he couldn't wait to
see what she had on under the conspicuous trench.

"I hear it's been a tough day. Hell, a tough week
for you. How about you let me make it better?" She
winked and undid the belt on her coat.

He licked his lips and slid his hand down over his
shorts, giving himself a stroke before squeezing the
base of his cock so he wouldn't come right there with
just the promise of her.

"I think you being here at all makes it better."

Her eyes went from sensual to surprised back to
sensual in a blink. He liked that he'd surprised her
and knew he was going to fucking *love* this particular
surprise of hers.

Slowly, she pulled the flaps away on her coat and
spread her arms, her hands holding each side of the
coat.

He went to his knees without even thinking about it. "Thank you, thank you, thank you." He whispered the words, and Jillian laughed, her eyes dancing.

"Well, I brought the great Wes Montgomery to his knees. I think my work here is done."

He narrowed his eyes. "You better not leave yet, woman. Show me everything you've got."

She tilted her head and cocked her hip. "Everything, big boy?"

He swallowed hard. "Everything."

She wore a set of red and black garters with tiny bows on the front over matching panties that rode low on her hips and thigh-high, lace-top stockings. Her bra was one of those demi ones that lifted her breasts so it looked like they lay on red and black lacy clouds, overfilling the cups and begging for his mouth.

The best part, though, was the fact that she wore a tool belt over it all, with a wrench on one side and a measuring tape on the other.

She slowly pulled the measuring tape out of her belt and pulled the tape out, her tongue between her teeth.

"Before I ask you what you're going to measure with that, should I ask what the wrench is for?" he asked, his cock impossibly hard.

Jillian rolled her eyes. "Because I'm a plumber, and I was going to make a pipe joke, but then I decided I'd *measure* things instead. The wrench is just for show."

He snorted. "Thank God. I wasn't quite sure I was ready to see what you'd want to wrench."

She winced but pulled out more of the measuring tape. "And what about this? I wonder what I could possibly measure..."

He moved forward then, needing her close. "Well, come on, Jilli. Let's see what you've got." He kissed her then, taking his time exploring her mouth and her taste. She leaned into him, their bodies aligning even better now that she was in her heels. "I've never seen you in heels," he murmured against her neck.

"I'm more comfortable in jeans and boots, but sometimes I like feeling sexy."

He pulled back slightly so he could wrap his hand around the back of her neck. "You're sexy in your boots. Sexy in your flats that you wear when you let me take you out on a date. You're just fucking sexy, Jillian."

She licked her lips, her hands digging into his hips. "You sound like you're spouting Dr. Seuss for adults."

He snorted before biting down on her neck. "Oh, yeah? Maybe we could go into a new business."

"Dirty poems? I don't know. I might have to see how dirty you can get first before I dare try that partnership."

He slid his hand under her open jacket and around to her butt. His fingers splayed under the tiny scrap of lace of her thong and played with the crack of her ass. She shivered in his hold.

"I know you have an idea of what you want tonight. Want to fill me in?" He slid the coat off her shoulders before going back to molding her ass in his hands. She was so fit and worked hard on her legs because of her job. He loved her ass. There was just enough that it jiggled when he fucked her from behind and gave him something nice to hold onto when he slammed her down on top of him.

"I want you," she whispered. "I want to see how far you can go, Wesley. Think you can do that?"

He rocked into her. "Go into the bedroom and get comfortable. I need to get a few things. And then, Jillian?" She met his gaze. "Then I think we'll push each other. That's something I know we can do. We're good at it."

She leaned forward and bit his lip—something she was able to do since she was wearing heels—before licking away the sting.

"Fuck me hard tonight. Make me come. Hell, make me pass out because I'm so sated. Then we'll see if we've pushed each other hard enough."

And with that, she turned again and swayed to the bedroom, her ass looking so fucking bitable in that thong he had to take a few deep breaths so he didn't accidentally rub one off right there in his living room. He almost thought about it, however. That way, he'd be able to take the edge off and last longer for her.

She'd rocked his world in more ways than one, apparently.

After he shook his head to clear the lust riding him past the brink of sanity, he quickly went to his kitchen to gather a few things. He'd never done this exact thing before, but he'd read about it in one of Jillian's books and now wanted to try it.

Jillian lay in the middle of his bed propped up on pillows when he walked inside. She'd taken off her heels but still wore her lace number.

"I kind of miss the heels," he said as he set down the metal bowl of ice, a warm, wet towel, and a dry one.

She raised a brow at his goodies from the kitchen before looking at him. "I thought about it, but knowing me, I'd puncture skin or your mattress. Plus, I know you, and you're not a shoes-in-the-bedroom kind of guy. Hell, I'm surprised you let me wear them past the entryway."

He laughed, shaking his head as he knelt on the bed. "Well, that much is actually true." He kissed one knee, then the next. Her legs parted automatically, and he swallowed hard. "You know me well."

"I try. Though I never thought I would when we first met."

"Fighting's foreplay for some," he agreed, using his knuckle to trace a line down her inner thigh. Goosebumps pebbled on her flesh, and he licked a path down them.

"I'll yell at you later," she breathed.

He winked and moved back before brushing his thumb over her heat, her lace panties already drenched. He bent down and kissed her cunt right through the fabric, loving the way she moaned. When he lifted up slightly to unclip her garters and grip the edge of her thong, she let out a shuddering breath.

"You'll be the death of me, Wes Montgomery." She moaned again when he removed and tossed her thong to the side and buried his face between her legs. She tasted so damn sweet, he knew if he weren't careful, he'd spend the rest of the evening eating her out until they both passed out from pleasure.

He licked her again and sat up, watching her as she looked up from under hooded eyes.

"What's the ice for?"

"It's a hot day, and you were in a trench coat. I figured some ice could help." He reached for one of the ice cubes and licked it slowly.

"Damn," she said on a laugh. "That's way too sexy for me."

"Oh, yeah?" He bent forward and blew on her clit. Her hips rocked off the bed, and he clucked his tongue. "Keep yourself steady. Ass on the bed and legs spread. If you don't keep it like that, I'll stop you from coming and just jerk off watching you—which could also be sexy as fuck."

"Dirty, dirty boy. I like it." She wiggled down into the pillows, gripped the bedspread tightly and spread her legs even wider.

He lowered himself even more and pressed the ice cube against her clit.

"Wes! That's fucking cold."

He chuckled roughly before moving the ice so he could blow warm air over her clit. Then he licked her, sucking on her tight nub before going back to her with the ice. He repeated the process over and over until the ice was fully melted and her legs were shaking around his head.

"I need you, Wes," she whispered. "For the love of God, if you don't get inside me and fuck me hard into this mattress, I'm going to burn up right here."

"I need a condom," he growled out, so hard he knew he wouldn't last long. "One sec."

"No, you don't. We're both tested and showed each other the results, *and* I have an IUD. Get. Inside. Me."

Now he *knew* he'd burst. Just the thought of being bare inside her... Damn.

He moved everything out of the way, knowing he'd have more to play with later with the towels and the rest of the ice that hadn't melted if they wanted, and went to sit between her legs. Somehow, he'd tugged off his shorts, and she'd taken off her bra, but she still wore her garters and a wide smile.

"You're so fucking beautiful."

And he loved her.

But he couldn't say that. Not yet. They were still new, still figuring out who they were with each other and not just in their worlds. Yet he pushed that out of his mind and lowered himself over her, taking her mouth as she reached between them. When her hands gripped his cock, he growled.

"I'm going to come if you keep touching me."

"Then fuck me, Wesley."

He bit her shoulder, and she groaned. "That I can do." She guided him to her entrance, and he met her gaze as he entered her inch by slow inch. They clung to one another, rising in the heat and meeting thrust for thrust. Their hands explored their bodies as their mouths moved from kisses and licks, to bites and groans.

And when she came around him, he followed, knowing he wouldn't have been able to last beyond the tight vice of her pussy coming around him. His body shook, and his balls tightened almost to the point of pain, but when they were both able to finally breathe, he held her close, knowing he'd never be able to let her go.

He hadn't been expecting to fall for his brother's ex. Hadn't been expecting to fall for the woman who constantly pushed his buttons. And yet, here he was, in love with a woman he couldn't quite read, so he didn't know how she felt about him. Yet with her arms around him and her lips on his as they lazily kissed as the moon rose high in the sky, he couldn't quite care. Being with her pushed all thoughts of what-ifs, the stress from the day, the fact that no one knew who had attacked him in that alley, and the little things that kept coming up at work and in his life out of his mind.

With her in his arms, he could forget everything else.

And for once, he was just fine with that.

CHAPTER EIGHTEEN

J illian wiped the sweat from her brow and packed up another box from her father's place. Her heart hurt, and her body ached after only two hours of boxing up and sorting things. The estate and house were now in her name, and she'd already had the meeting with her father's lawyer and the reading of the will.

She shivered at the memory of that meeting. Though the elderly man had tried to be nice, she'd felt so alone, so *cold* reading that her father had left everything to her. There hadn't been any surprises, but she still had to listen to it and nod along. She'd gone alone, though Wes, Storm, and their parents had offered to come and be by her side.

Jillian was going to take her time with everything that came next, however. Her father had already been at her to go through boxes because he wanted her to have what was hers while he was still there to see her face. Now...well, now she would keep at it and hope that he was up there somewhere, watching her but in far less pain.

She sniffed and then leaned into Wes's hard chest when he wrapped his arms around her waist.

"We can stop for the day, baby," he whispered. It was the Sunday after their Friday-night ice and heat fest in his bedroom, and they'd spent every moment together since. She wasn't sure when they'd gone from testing the waters out to full-blown couple on the verge of something she couldn't quite name, but she knew it was important.

"I know. I'm just trying to sort for charities and things that could be useful for Roger or any of Dad's friends."

"And you have time." He kissed the back of her neck, and she sighed.

Time. That was one thing she'd thought she had so much of at one point. But when she lost her dad, she'd stopped believing that.

"I guess I'm just tired," she said after a moment.

"We both had a long week, and have another long week ahead of us. What do you say we drive out to Golden and go for a hike? Just a short one without too many hills. Just a relaxing stroll where we can get out of buildings and boxes."

She turned in his arms and rested her head on his chest. "I think that sounds like a great plan." She leaned on him more than she thought she would. Hell, she leaned on him more than she'd leaned on anyone in as long as she could remember.

The thing of it was, he didn't force her into it. He was there if she needed him, but he didn't prop her up as if she couldn't do it herself. He understood that sometimes she needed to stand on her own two feet and didn't push. And when he was too tired and angry with work or family, he leaned on her, too.

They were finding their balance, and it was thrilling...and scary.

They needed to talk about their relationship soon, she knew, or she'd worry herself into a corner.

Because it had started out as a way to relieve tension, to let the spark of attraction burn its course, but now, she wasn't sure. She wouldn't worry about it today, however. Today, she would push those thoughts from her mind and just *be*.

She didn't know if she could handle anything else.

Wes helped her put away the box she'd been working on, and the two of them headed out to his truck and then off to Golden. It really wouldn't be a mountain hike, more of a tiny foothill hike, but as it was around lunchtime, it was already too late in the day to start one of those. They picked up food on the way and ate in the car, their conversation quiet and about nothing too serious. With all the seriousness going on, sometimes it was nice to talk about anything but the important things. That time would come later.

The Rockies seriously took her breath away every time she truly looked at them. While sometimes they became a backdrop to the city where she hardly noticed them; other times, she actually looked up and realized how blessed she was to live where she did. Not everyone saw mountains like these in their lives. And only a fraction of those got to live near them.

There were simply no words to describe the beauty of it. The mountains reached high into the sky, and she honestly couldn't believe how large they were. They just kept going and going, the masterpiece of Earth's beauty unveiled right before her. Trees and bushes filled her vision, rocks and streams surrounding her, and yet she felt as if she weren't alone even with the idea of no one around her. She couldn't be alone with the world surrounding her such as it was.

They walked hand-in-hand down the trail, her body finally feeling slightly lighter once she breathed in the fresh air and leaned into Wes's strong hold. Once again, she was leaning, yet it was okay—for now.

"It feels good to be out here," Wes said once they got to a clearing where they could sit on a couple of boulders. "I haven't been up here in far too long. Hell, between work and family, I think the only nature I've seen is in my backyard."

She snorted. "Well, you *do* have a particularly amazing backyard for a man who lives in the suburbs."

He snorted and handed over one of the water bottles they'd picked up with their lunch. "The land was the reason I got the house. The lot's about twice as big as any of the others around me, so it's my own little paradise without having to go very far. The house itself sucked when I moved in over a decade ago, but between my family and me, we've fixed it up to where I want it. The barn's the only thing left until I get the notion to redo it all or something."

"Why do you have such a big house for just you?" she asked, not looking at him but the trees and paths around them. As he was doing the same, it was quite nice and relaxing.

He let out a breath and leaned back on the boulder. "Well, I didn't think I'd still be by myself at this age."

She glanced at him out of the corner of her eye. "You say that like you're an old man or something. You're not anywhere close to being old, Wes."

"True, but I'm also not in my twenties or even early thirties anymore. I'm the last Montgomery without a wife or thinking about kids. Though I don't know if Autumn and Griffin are planning to have them or not. They said in the past that they like being the fun aunt and uncle." He shot her a look. "I'm not saying this because I'm trying to have a deep conversation about us, by the way. I'm just telling you why I bought that house."

She nodded, understanding. "I thought I'd be married and working on a family by now, too." She shrugged, and he reached out to tangle his fingers with hers. The connection steadied her, which was weird because holding hands with anyone else hadn't done that before. "I spent a lot of my twenties building my career and hiding behind my so-called relationship with Storm."

"You're barely thirty, Jillian." His tone was dry, but there was still an understanding in his gaze.

She rolled her eyes. "True, but I can't say I'm in my twenties anymore. Not that I particularly liked that era. I'm not that far into my thirties, like you said, but I already like them more. I know who I am, what I want, and I'm working on getting there. I don't feel like I need to be apologetic anymore for loving my job and being damn good at it."

"Hell no. You're the best damn plumber we've ever had."

She tipped her imaginary hat. "Why thank you, sir." They both laughed, and she wiped her hands on her jeans, calmer than she had been before. "I don't think any of us truly found the path we needed until it was right in front of us, you know? We might have tried to pave other roads, or at least the ones that we thought were good for us, but I think, at least the two of us, found one that worked for us rather than what might have worked for others.

"I thought I'd marry Sophia," Wes said after a moment. She froze fractionally before she made herself relax. While she might not like hearing about his ex, he saw *hers* every day and seemed to be fine with it. She could deal with a little conversation.

"When I bought the house, she and I were seeing each other and getting serious. Yes, I bought the place for myself but also with room for family. I didn't make any of the major remodeling decisions until she and I were no longer seeing each other. I waited, I guess, for input from the woman who was going to be my wife, and in the end, that didn't happen."

"She hurt you." There was no hiding the truth of that in his tone, but there was a sense of finality about it, as well.

"Yeah, and pissed me off. She left me for a man with deeper pockets to help along her gambling habits and any other addictions she picked up along the way. I enabled her at first because I thought that was what I was supposed to do. I thought I was helping everything by fixing it all, only in the end, I made it worse. It took me a while to realize that."

"You're a fixer," she said, understanding. "You've always been that way. Storm told me some," she explained when he gave her a look. "How even when you were younger, you tried to figure out how to make things better for your siblings so your parents wouldn't have to worry."

Wes gave her a grin. "Maya really wanted her lemonade and sticker stand to work out, and boys kept coming up and trying to steal her favorite stickers. So when she punched the neighbor boy in the mouth for stealing, I tried to take the fall for it, but Maya would have none of it. She told our parents straight out what she'd done and that she'd do it again. And when that boy's mom came to yell at our parents for raising a heathen girl, they stood up for all of us. Yeah, Maya got grounded for using her fists, but they didn't yell at her for defending her territory."

He smiled at the memory, and she couldn't help but imagine little Maya with pigtails, scowling at anyone who would dare steal from her. Then, of course, she pictured a slightly older teenage Wes, glaring down at anyone who thought to hurt his baby sister. It was a cute image, and she bet he'd do it again even now that they were all far older.

"I don't miss Sophia, by the way," Wes added after a moment, surprising her.

"What?"

He turned so they were facing each other, their hands still clasped together. "I don't miss her. I did at one point, but seeing her again so recently? It just reminds me how much work it was to be with her. And loving someone shouldn't be work, not really. A relationship *is* work, that much I know. It *should* have both people working on it to make sure that the other person knows they're all in. But the actual love? That shouldn't be work. And for Sophia, it was work." He winced and leaned down to kiss Jillian's temple. "And I probably shouldn't be talking about her, huh? Kills the mood."

She shook her head. "You should talk about whatever is on your mind. I'm not hurt that you're talking about her. It gives me more insight into who you are." She shrugged. "If we ignore the tough topics, then what we have is only superficial."

He tilted his head and studied her. "And what do we have, Jillian?"

She swallowed hard, annoyed with herself for broaching this topic though she knew she'd needed to. "I don't know what to call it."

He laughed and squeezed her hand. "Sounds about like what I'm thinking, too. Are we too old for boyfriends and girlfriends? Maybe, but calling you anything other than my girlfriend sounds weird." He leaned forward and cupped her face with his free and. "I like you, Jillian. I like being with you. I like the way you make me feel. I like the fact that we're learning each other even when us being together at all was unexpected. I don't know what's coming next for us, but I do know that I want to find out. Together."

She licked her lips and leaned forward to kiss his lips softly. "I want to find out, too. I didn't expect this. Didn't expect you. I mean, I don't think we had a real conversation without snark or yelling until we were making out."

Wes's eyes filled with laughter. "True, though I'm glad we still snark and possibly yell. Keeps things interesting."

Her phone buzzed with a weather alert, and she sighed. "Looks like rain is on its way. We should head back."

"Want to come to my place? I'll cook."

"Words any girl likes to hear," she said with a laugh as they made their way down the path. The two of them had been very careful not to use the L-word when they were talking about their feelings, and she wasn't really sure if that's what she felt for him. She liked Wes. She wanted to be with him. But love? Well, love hurt. A lot. It was such a risk—especially for her in this situation. Because if she truly loved Wes and it became too much work like he'd said had happened with Sophia, then she'd be left with no one.

She'd lose her friends, she'd lose the foundation she'd tried to make for herself.

She'd lose Wes.

So taking it slowly like they were, would have to be enough. Because loving Wes right now would be a mistake.

And if she kept telling herself that, she might one day believe it.

"Did they ever find out who tried to break into the warehouse," Jillian asked as they hiked back, trying to keep her mind off of her and Wes's future.

"No, and it's pissing me off. We've had what? *Five* failed attempts? I can see blaming kids for maybe one or two of those times, but all of them? I just don't know. We've been set back twice now because of broken glass and knocked over supplies, and I'm really fucking annoyed. Not to mention the elevator breaking down *again* after we fixed it. And the random leaks going on in the building that have nothing to do with your work," he added quickly when she growled. "All of that added up together sounds like either someone is out to sabotage this project, or we're cursed."

"Don't forget you getting hurt," she said, her voice cracking when she remembered the look of him in that hospital bed. "You got jumped right after we started this project, and that guy kept asking where it was. What is *it*"?

Wes frowned. "You don't think the two are connected, do you?"

She shook her head. "No, not really, but you never know." She froze as she remembered something she'd forgotten to tell Wes.

"What is it?" he asked, stopping to face her. He looked her over and frowned. "Are you hurt? Is it your ankle? I'll carry you back."

She held up her hand as he bent to pick her up. "I'm not hurt, Mr. Fixer. I just had a thought. I'm really okay."

He kissed her quickly. "Maybe I just wanted to get my hands on you."

"Cheeky. And maybe when we get back to your place..."

"That's a promise." He spanked her, and she shivered. Damn man. "What was your thought?"

"After I got home one night, I briefly thought someone had gone through my things. I can't explain it, but it was as if someone had been in my house and I just *knew*. I mean, I chalked it up to me being tired and paranoid at the time, but now, I'm not so sure."

"Fuck, Jilli. Are you serious? Why didn't you tell me when it happened? Or call the cops?"

She held out her hands again, annoyed at herself and him in the moment. "I don't remember why I didn't mention it at the time, probably because I was exhausted, but it honestly slipped my mind because it didn't seem like a big deal. And nothing was out of place, so it's not like I could call the cops and say 'hey, I feel weird, can you use your manpower for the little woman in need?'"

Wes let out a growl and cursed under his breath. "If you thought someone was in your house looking for something and not finding it, it could be connected to everything else going on."

"Or we've been watching too many crime shows where *everything* is connected. It was just a feeling. I shouldn't have brought it up. The only reason I did was because I forgot about it in the first place. I'm sure nothing is connected. It wouldn't make sense if it were."

He narrowed his eyes, and she tugged on his hand. The first crack of thunder splintered the air, and she tugged harder. "Come on, we're *so* close to the truck, and I don't want to get drenched." He reluctantly ran beside her as they made their way to the vehicle. The first drops of rain splashed the windshield as soon as they got inside and started the engine.

She knew he was stewing over what she'd told him, and she was doing the same, but really, what were the odds that it was all connected? Slim, she reminded herself.

Plus, it wasn't like she had anything anyone would want.

Right?

CHAPTER NINETEEN

"We're going to be late," Wes said as he leaned against the door in his bedroom, and Jillian knelt in front of him, her hand slowly sliding up and down his cock. It was such a pretty picture that he knew he'd always be able to imagine her on her knees, holding him by the balls—literally—and having all the control.

It was damn sexy.

"I think we have time for me to finish what I'm doing before we go." She winked before using her tongue to play with the slit at the top of his cock.

He groaned and fisted his hand in her hair. "Okay, okay. I guess if you want to suck me off, we'll find the time."

She squeezed him, and he let out a laughing wheeze. "That's what I thought, Wesley." Then she hummed along his shaft as she sucked him down, bobbing her head and making his eyes cross.

Her tongue slid along his length as she worked him over, bringing him closer and closer to the edge but pulling back when he was almost there. She knew his body, knew the signs for when he was about to come and was *empowered* because of it.

And he fucking loved it.

Because when he took her later, he'd do the same to her, knowing her body in and out and bringing them both pleasure because *they* found it together, driving them both past the brink of obsession and pleasure.

His jeans were still on his hips, just riding low with his fly open as she hollowed her cheeks. He groaned, coming down her throat in the next instant. He'd tugged on her hair to warn her, but she'd just hummed along, swallowing every drop of him. And when she let go of his dick with a pop, he grunted and tugged her up by the hair, aggressive yet gentle because he knew that was how she liked it. He crushed his mouth to hers, tasting himself on her tongue. It made him hard again, and as she squirmed in his hold, clearly turned on by giving him a blowjob, he tightened his grip on her hip and hair, exploring her mouth to get his fill.

"Wes," she gasped, breaking away from him as they both fought to catch their breaths.

"You're so fucking hot." He bit her lip, and she moaned.

She winked when she pulled back, wiping the drop of come they'd both missed from the side of her mouth. Seeing the wicked glint in her eye, he decided to take control—just for now.

He turned them both and twisted her around until her back was to his front. Then he pressed her hard into the door, loving the way her pulse raced beneath his hand as he held onto her wrist. When she pressed her cheek to the door and wiggled her ass against his raging hard-on, he slapped her butt hard.

"Don't move," he ordered, his voice low. "You don't have the upper hand here, Jilli. I'm going to fuck this pussy—*my* pussy—but before I do, I'm going to see how wet you are. Are you a dirty, girl, Jillian? Are you wet because you had my dick in your mouth, choking you as I came?"

She licked her lips, obviously turned on at his words. But because they were going a little farther than they had before, he leaned forward and nipped at her ear.

"You tell me to stop, I stop," he whispered. "I go too far, you tell me, and we stop this right now. I'm not going to hurt you, but I'm going to make you beg for it." They never ventured into anything too kinky where a safe-word would be needed, since that's not what they preferred in their relationship, but he always wanted to make sure the two of them were on the same page just in case.

She smiled at him, her eyes warming. "I like it, Wes. Don't worry about me, just make me feel good."

He leaned down and took her lips. "That I can do. Now, let me check this pussy. Are you wet? Or are you just lying to me when you say you're turned on."

Wes undid the button on her jeans and slid his hand down the front of her pants. It was a tight fit, but he had his palm over her mound and his fingers stuffed inside her in no time. Her cunt clenched around his fingers, and he grinned.

"So. Fucking. Wet." He pumped in and out of her a couple of times, letting her grow accustomed to his hand, then sped up. The wet sounds of him fingering her filled the room, and it made him even hornier. Holy hell, his woman was too hot for words, and he loved the way they went at it during sex.

"I'm close," she panted.

He leaned forward and bit her shoulder over her shirt. She let her head fall back as she came, her pussy like a vice around his fingers as she tightened around him. He slowly removed his hand as she came down off her high and then made sure she was watching as he licked her juices off his hand.

"Holy hell, that's hot," she said with a laugh. "I never thought that was sexy when I watched porn, but you doing it? Just...get inside me already, will you? Because I think I need that big dick of yours right now."

He laughed, loving that they *laughed* and joked together during sex. She helped him with her pants and then shoved his pants down to his knees, but he kept her in the same position so he could take her from behind.

"Hands on the door," he ordered, and when she complied, he entered her. She was so wet and slick, he knew neither one of them would last long, but he didn't mind. Their foreplay was always so long and hot that they usually could go at it three or four times a night if they played it right.

The door rocked on its hinges as he fucked her hard, her hips moving with him and pressing into his groin so she went deeper and deeper. Too soon, they were both coming and panting each other's names. Sweat covered their bodies, and he knew they were both sticky and messy.

Seriously the best sex. Ever.

"We're officially going to be late to dinner," Jillian said on a laugh, her face still pressed against the door.

He rolled his eyes and smacked her bare bottom that now held a nice pink spot, so he rubbed it softly so it wouldn't ache.

"I told you that before you started sucking me."

"Well, you didn't put up much of a fight, did you?"

"You had my dick in your mouth, I couldn't really come up with an argument. Now let's clean up and head out. A little late is okay." Something he'd never said before in his life.

Needless to say, their shower together took longer than planned, and a little late turned into a whole lot late but the hostess with the knowing glint in her eye had seated them at their table anyway.

"I saw the way she looked at you," Jillian whispered over her menu. "She knew what we were doing."

He smiled and studied the drink specials and what was on tap. "Well, since you're wearing two different shoes and your dress isn't fully zipped, I'm not surprised."

She gasped and checked herself before kicking him under the table with her very pointy shoe—the same shoe that had a matching one on her other foot.

"Liar," she whispered fiercely.

"But you laughed." He winked, and she laughed and flipped him off from behind her menu.

"I can't believe how nice this week was compared to the last," Jillian said once they had finished their dinner and were now onto their chocolate tortes. Wes ate his slowly, his attention on the way she licked her whipped cream from her fork rather than what the dessert tasted like.

He was seriously a goner.

"You're right," he said after he took another bite. He needed to keep his mind on their conversation and not on what he planned to do later. "We actually got work done and are heading toward our target. It was a good week."

There had been no mishaps, no break-ins, and no leads on who had jumped Wes in that alley. His ribs ached just thinking about it, but he'd had no long-term effects from the incident. They'd even called the detective in charge about Jillian's place but had pretty much been blown off. In the grand scheme of things, it wouldn't make sense that everything was connected, but they'd wanted to make sure there was a record of it nonetheless.

"Here's to next week," Jillian said, tapping her fork to his.

"Speaking of next week, Mom called and told me we're doing the family dinner at her place on Saturday. We alternate months with Austin since his house is big enough to fit all of us."

"Your house is, too," she added.

"True, but we're only just now adding Austin into the rotation. Give it time to trickle down," he said on a laugh. "Anyway, do you want to come? It's an invite from me, by the way. I want to bring you as my date, rather than my mother inviting you like last time."

Her eyes brightened. "I'd love to, and you know your mom is probably going to call tomorrow and invite me anyway. She's so sweet like that."

And a matchmaker, but that was besides the point. "She will. She likes you." And wanted to make sure Jillian never felt alone. He understood and loved that his family had taken to her so quickly.

He had too, after all.

He loved Jillian Reid. And one day soon, he'd tell her. She wasn't ready, and they both knew that. He'd seen the look in her eyes when they talked about their relationship, and he knew if he told her and she ran, she'd feel as though she were alone even if that weren't the case. Plus, she was still healing over her father, and they weren't that far into their own relationship. When the time was right, he'd tell her.

Or when he found the courage...you know, whatever.

"Are you ready to head back to your place?" she asked once the waiter came back with Wes's card.

He nodded, then froze. "Holy...oh my God."

"What?" she straightened, her eyes on alert. "What's wrong?"

"I forgot my tablet at the warehouse. I can't believe I did that."

She blinked. "You? *You* forgot your tablet? That thing is *always* on you. Like I was surprised you didn't sleep with it. And it's Saturday, Wes. That means it's been over twenty-four hours since you last looked at it."

"I can't quite believe it." He'd been so into his date and time with Jillian that he'd actually focused on life rather than work. Hell had well and truly frozen over.

"Well, we can stop by the warehouse on the way to your place. It's sort of on the way."

He shook his head. "It can wait until Monday," he lied.

"Sure, Wes. And then we'll see a pretty night rainbow once we get home. Come on. You know you won't be able to truly focus now that you know you forgot it. Before, you couldn't dwell because you didn't realize, but now that you do? It'll always be in the back of your mind, and I'm not really digging the idea of getting it on while you're reminiscing about time with your pretty tablet."

She fluttered her eyelashes as she stood, and Wes broke out into a loud laugh, catching the attention of a few of the other patrons.

"Come on, then," he said, taking her hand. "Hopefully, it won't take too long because now I'm having images of you, me, and my tablet." He leaned down to her ear and whispered, "We'll put on some porn and see if we can figure out the moves."

They were still laughing as they made it to his car and slid in. They'd left their trucks at his place and taken his car since they wanted to be fancy for the night. It was nice shedding their work boots and jeans and putting on something soft and glittery in Jillian's case.

"What kind of porn are we talking about?" Jillian asked, her hand clasped in his as he drove.

He shifted in his seat, his cock hard already. It was apparently a perpetual case when he was around her these days. "I was thinking the porn for women category. They always have the best oral that leads to sex where they both get off."

"Rather than a forty-minute blowjob, a couple fake screams, then his coming on her face?" she asked dryly.

"Sounds about right." He paused. "Or wrong. Plus, how the hell does a man last forty minutes like that? I barely last two when you're giving me a blowjob."

She laughed and leaned over the console to kiss his cheek. "You last longer than two minutes, Wesley, but it does make me all warm and tingly inside that I can get you off."

"Ditto," he growled. "Now let's stop talking about sex because I'm having trouble keeping my eyes on the road."

"Well, I can talk about the snake's nest I found in one of the walls of my old job. The momma had left her skin behind, and oh dear Lord, that snake must have been big. But the babies? There were like twenty of them making little sounds as they slithered in that wall." She shuddered. "I thought it was just a bad clog at first, but nope, snakes. Lots of them."

Wes shuddered, his hand gripping the steering wheel just a bit tighter. "What did you do with the snakes?" he asked through clenched teeth. He wasn't afraid of snakes, per se, but a bunch of them together? No thanks.

"Animal control came and relocated the babies. Not sure if they ever found the momma, though. I was done with the job by then and didn't hear."

They pulled into the site and parked under one of the big lights that lit up the warehouse. "Thanks for that mental image."

"I helped though, right?"

"You did something. Want to wait here while I run to where I probably left the damn thing?"

She shook her head and started to get out of the car as her answer. "I'm fine. It's a warm night, and I don't want to stay alone in the car. Plus...I know you called security to say you'd be by, but I'd still rather be with you."

At the mention of why they had security to begin with, his jaw clenched. "Let's get to it," he said and held out his hand. She took it, and they walked to the security station, checked in, and then headed to the warehouse.

"I think I left it near where I set up my office. I'm such a fucking idiot."

"No, you're not, and you have everything on your phone anyway, but let's just get it and head out. This place kind of gives me the creeps in the dark."

He wrapped his arm around her shoulder and pulled her close. "Don't worry, I'll protect you." And he wasn't lying.

"Not if I protect you first." And he had a feeling she wasn't lying either.

They made their way to where he'd been working on Friday afternoon, and he let out a relieved breath when he spotted his tablet hanging out on a stack of wood, untouched and lonely.

"Hello, my precious," Jillian whispered. He gave her a look, and she blinked innocently. "I was just narrating your internal monologue."

He kissed her hard. "And that's why I love you." They both froze as he said the words, and her eyes widened. "Uh..."

But before he could say anything else, there was a sound behind them. They both turned, confused, then everything happened at once.

A bright light flashed in front of him, and what sounded like fireworks popped all around them. Jillian pressed into his side, and he tried to cover her but hit the ground instead. His head slammed into the cement, and Jillian's did the same.

He turned so he covered her body, and his hand slipped in something warm and wet. When his brain finally caught up to the red in his vision, he choked and pressed his hand to Jillian's shoulder where blood seeped over her black, sparkly dress and pooled beneath them.

Her eyes were closed, her face paling, and he couldn't think of what to do next. He turned to look over his shoulder as four big men raised their guns toward them. He didn't move, he didn't breathe, but before he could register that this might be the last moment of his life, another shot echoed in the room.

"Freeze! This is the police! We have you surrounded. Put down your weapons and put your hands up."

Wes's hands shook as he covered Jillian's wound. He needed to get her to the hospital. He knew this was bad, knew there wasn't much time to waste.

And then everything changed again.

A black blur shoved into him, and shots rang out again. He hit the ground hard on his shoulder, and a big man landed on top of him. He didn't know at first if it was a cop or whoever had attacked them, but he didn't care, not in the heat of the moment when he needed to be with Jillian.

He shoved the guy off him and sat up, finally seeing it was a man in a black mask and clothes. Knowing this couldn't be a cop, Wes punched the guy hard in the face, once, twice, three times until he was down for the count, before crawling over to where Jillian lay so still he feared the worst.

People shouted around him, but he could only look at the woman he loved, dying in his arms. He couldn't fathom a world where he didn't hear her laugh, didn't see her smile.

"I need help," he called out. "Someone call an ambulance."

Others moved around him then, and he recognized one of them as Frances. She had a large first aid kit in one hand, and two cops were by her side. He let them push him to the side but still kept his hand on Jillian's as they worked to keep her stable until the ambulance arrived.

His body ached, and his heart raced. He couldn't focus on anything, and it wasn't until someone came to his side and touched the back of his head that he realized he was bleeding.

They shined a light in his eyes and tugged Jillian away as his world went black.

He couldn't lose her.

He couldn't imagine his world without her.

He couldn't.

CHAPTER TWENTY

Jillian blinked under the harsh lights as she woke. She didn't know how long she'd been asleep, but she knew where she was.

A hospital.

She'd been shot.

Or at least...that's what it felt like. Either that or a Mack truck had slammed into her head-on and had left her bleeding and cold on the cement floor of the warehouse. She couldn't quite remember everything that had happened, and for all she knew, she'd imagined the searing pain in her shoulder and the nauseating thump her head had made against the floor when she fell. She knew she was forgetting something important, but she couldn't quite remember.

Beeps and other hospital sounds filled her ears as her eyes struggled to adjust to the bright overhead lights. Her throat ached, and her body felt so heavy that she was afraid she'd never be able to lift her arms again. Of course, as soon as she tried, a searing pain arched along her shoulder, and she stifled a gasp.

Someone next to her shuffled closer and sucked in a breath. "Jillian? You're awake. Oh, thank God."

She knew that voice.

Wes.

She'd jumped in front of him and had been shot, but if he were talking to her, he had to be okay, right? Because she didn't know what she'd do if he'd been hurt.

"Wes?" she croaked.

"Hold on, let me get you some water." He moved away, and she kept blinking so he wouldn't be a dark blur above her head. He put a straw to her lips just as her vision came into focus, and she could have cried at the sight of him.

He honestly looked like hell, but she'd never found him sexier.

Because he was *there.*

She swallowed a few sips of water before he pulled the cup away and set it down on a table next to the bed.

"I'm going to go call the nurse to let her know you're awake," he said softly, leaning over her. "But I'm so fucking glad your eyes are open right now, Jillian. You scared the crap out of me, and when you're fully alert, I plan to yell at you for daring to scare years off my life."

He traced his finger along her jaw, and she whimpered, tears falling down her cheeks. What was with her? She wasn't such a crier, yet just the touch of him sent her into emotional turmoil.

"Be right back, baby." Then he was gone, and she was alone again, wondering what the hell had actually happened. He wasn't out of the room long, however. She blinked, and suddenly, he was there again at her side, along with two nurses and perhaps even a doctor to check on her.

"The bullet didn't hit any bone," the doctor explained. "That's a good thing, but you lost a lot of blood on scene and have a concussion. However, with time and physical therapy on that shoulder of yours, you're going to feel like new again in no time." He explained a few other things before leaving to go talk to another patient. One of the nurses stayed behind to tell her about the call button and what she could do while in bed, as well as instructing that she had to stay in the hospital for at least two more days under observation.

After what felt like hours, she was finally alone with Wes and had no idea what she was going to say.

"What happened?" Okay, so maybe her mouth was working a little faster than her brain at the moment.

He gave her a small smile before taking the stool next to the bed and sitting close. He held her hand in his, his brow furrowed.

"You almost died because you pushed me out of the way of a freaking bullet. That's what happened."

She swallowed hard, the memory of the flash and echoing bang reverberating in her skull. That wasn't something she would forget anytime soon, but she'd talk about that with him later. She already had a feeling that every time she closed her eyes, she'd see the shot, feel the pain again, but Wes was here. He was *alive*. And because of that, she could get through the aftereffects if she needed to.

"I remember that part. Mostly."

"Then you'll remember this," Wes bit out. "Never. Ever. Do that again. I thought I'd lost you." His voice cracked, and he leaned forward to gently rest his forehead on hers. The action let her touch him without having to move, and for that, she was grateful.

"I could have lost you, too."

"I can't lose you, Jillian. I love you so damn much."

That's what she'd forgotten. Her eyes widened. "You said that to me," she whispered. "Right before everything went crazy."

He let out a shaky breath. "Yeah, not my brightest moment. I'd been waiting for the right time to tell you."

Tears filled her eyes, and she reached up with her uninjured arm to cup his cheek. "I love you, too," she whispered.

He smiled widely, his eyes glassy with unshed tears. "Yeah? That's good."

She laughed then and let out a groan since laughing hurt like hell. "Okay, no laughing for me."

His eyes narrowed this time, and he sat back down on the stool. "I'm never going to let you get hurt like this again."

"Wes, baby, you can't fix everything. I thought we went over this."

"Fine, then I'm not going to allow the *mob* to fucking shoot you again."

This time, she narrowed her eyes. "You're joking with me, right? There's a *mob* family in Denver?"

"Apparently, there's a mob family in lots of places outside of TV," Storm said as he strolled into the room, Everly by his side. "Sorry to interrupt, but the family is getting anxious in the waiting room, and we figured we'd be allowed in as the family of your fiancé and all."

Jillian must have hit her head harder than she thought. "My fiancé?" She looked over at Wes, whose cheeks had reddened.

"Uh...well...I was going to ask you in a few months, but that's besides the point."

"Huh?" Her heart raced. "Really?"

"What he means to say is, he refused to leave your side except when they were stitching up his head and when you were in surgery, and that meant he needed a way back to you since they only let family back here." Everly walked to the other side of the bed and leaned down to brush hair off Jillian's face. "Nice to see you awake, sleepy head. You scared the crap out of all of us."

"It's good to be awake," Jillian whispered before turning to Wes again. "And what does she mean stitch up your head? You're hurt? You should be lying down in a bed next to me, damn it. You'd better not have played hero and tried to shrug off any pain because you wanted to be here when I woke up."

Storm let out a strangled laugh, and Jillian watched as Everly glared at him. "Sorry," he said. "But it's kind of rich coming from you since you're the one who played hero, or so we hear." He held up his hands as he said it, but she'd seen the worry in his eyes.

He was still her best friend, even with all the things they'd put each other through, and for that, she'd always be grateful.

"I'm so confused. Can we take this step by step?" Jillian asked.

"We can do that," Wes whispered. "When we walked into the warehouse, apparently, we interrupted a search. It wasn't their first one either."

"Is this the mob you were talking about?" Jillian asked.

"As crazy as it sounds, yes," Everly said.

"It seems the building's owner prior to the previous one was the cousin—or maybe the second cousin?—of the current mob boss of Denver. They left a few things behind that they didn't realize were still hidden in the walls. This cousin wanted to take over the family business, as it were, and remembered that there were a few important documents that could incriminate not only him but also his family. I'm not a hundred percent clear on the details, but they needed to make sure we didn't find anything important. But it seems we might have."

"The box behind the water heater," Jillian said quickly. "The heavy one that we couldn't open."

"Got it in one. They came to the site because they didn't know we'd moved the box to another location. Hence the attack in the alley, the guy going through your house, and all of the break-ins at the site. They wanted to not only search the place for what they'd left behind, but they wanted to scare us away from the project."

"That's crazy," Jillian said. "Freaking crazy."

"And only a Montgomery could walk right into an insane story like that," Storm added dryly. "Seriously, this family is done with waiting rooms, you guys. We need to stop setting up camp in them."

"Wait. You mean they're all here? For me? Or was it because of Wes?" She turned to the man she loved again. "Because you still haven't told me how you got hurt."

Wes gripped her hand again, steadying her. It should have annoyed her that he could do that, but she never wanted to let him go again. "We'll get to that. And yes, the whole family—minus the kids, and probably one or two adults who tend to take shifts watching them—are outside waiting. For you. They already saw me after I got stitches on the back of my head. I'm just grateful they weren't staples."

"Tell me how you got hurt, Wesley, or I'm going to hurt you myself."

This time, Storm didn't bother to smother his laugh, and Everly joined in. "I like the two of you," her best friend said with a grin. "You both scared the daylights out of me, but you two together? I like."

"I'm so glad I have your approval," Jillian said drily before she once again turned to Wes. "Tell me, damn it."

"I hit my head when I fell and then again when one of the guys tackled me off of you. I hit him a few times and knocked him out before going back to you. I'm fine. Only a mild concussion and nowhere near as bad as you."

"Meaning when you both get out of here, you're taking it easy," Everly ordered. "I'm sure Marie and the rest of them already have a feeding and cleaning schedule for the two of you. Just go with it," Everly said directly to Jillian. "You're a Montgomery now, and you're just going to have to get used to the fact that you've been assimilated."

She stood up then and went to Storm's side. "We'll give you two a few minutes to talk before the horde comes in. As soon as you feel the slightest bit tired, Jillian, you tell us, and we'll all go. Okay?"

Jillian teared up again and gave her friend a wobbly smile. "I...I don't know what to say."

Storm wrapped his arm around Everly's shoulder and kissed the top of her head. "Welcome to the family."

And with that, the two of them left her and Wes alone. Her mind whirled, and she knew it would take a while for her to come to terms with everything that had happened, but she knew there was one thing she had to take care of before the rest of the Montgomerys came into her room.

"Were you serious before?" she asked, her voice carefully neutral.

He frowned and leaned over her again to run the back of his hand over her cheek. "When?"

"When you said you were going to ask me to marry you later rather than tell the nurses you already had."

His eyes widened, and she watched as his throat worked when he swallowed hard. "Yeah...I wasn't lying. I was going to wait until we found our rhythm as a couple and I finally found the guts to tell you that I loved you. Then I was going to get down on one knee and ask you to be my wife so we could spend the rest of our lives together. I don't even have a ring." He let out a rough laugh. "I was afraid to even look at what would suit you before I told you I loved you. I didn't want to scare you away."

And that did it. There she was, crying again. And from the look of panic on Wes's face, she'd surprised him with her tears.

"What is it? What's wrong?"

"I just love you so much," she said, and Wes laughed.

"You love me, so you're crying?"

She waved her good hand around her face. "I can't stop. It's probably the pain meds."

He just shook his head and kissed her brow. "Probably."

"Will you ask me?" she blurted.

He froze hovering over her. "Right now?"

"Yes, right now. I know you don't have a ring, and I can't exactly jump into your arms, but I think it's best not to lie to the doctors, right?"

His eyes filled with laughter, and a smile twitched at his lips. "Oh, yes? You want me to ask you to marry you, so you don't have to lie?"

"Well that, and I love you so freaking much. I've spent so long being afraid of what would happen when I looked for something more than what I used to think

I deserved. I wasted *so* much time without you in my life. I don't want to waste another second."

He leaned down and kissed her softly, ignoring what probably had to be horrible morning breath. "You took the words right out of my mouth. In fact, you pretty much said the perfect things for a proposal. I don't want to go home after this without you. I don't want to wake up again not knowing you're next to me, ready to spend the rest of our lives together."

She was fully crying now, and she saw the tears in his eyes, as well. "Come on, Wesley, don't leave me hanging."

He snorted and shook his head before bending slightly at the knee, but not fully going down to the ground since she was still in the bed. "Will you marry me, Jillian, and make me the happiest man on Earth? Will you fight with me and make up with me? Will you add more life to my too organized self and finally end my streak of being the only single Montgomery?"

She laughed and nodded. "We wouldn't want you to be the only single Montgomery in town for long. Yes, Wes, my Wesley, my Montgomery. I'll marry you. I'll be yours as you are mine. Now and always."

And when the nurses came into the room with Marie and Harry Montgomery, laughter and happy tears surrounded them, but Jillian only had eyes for Wes.

He was the one man she hadn't been looking for. The Montgomery she hadn't counted on. The Montgomery that was just for her.

Her Montgomery.

Forever.

MONTGOMERY EVER AFTER

Wes was one damn happy man. He had his arm around his newly healthy fiancée, a beer in his other hand, and his family surrounding him as they laughed and joked about stupid things that didn't really matter.

In a world where everything other than his family seemed to darken day-by-day, he'd take the laughs about nothing in particular to soothe his soul. He'd take the smiling eyes and the deep belly laughs of his father over the pain and near-death experiences almost all of them had experienced over the past few years.

His family was happy, healthy, and whole, and would probably be growing bigger in the next few years as his siblings either started or added to their families. Knowing the way he and Jillian were at it these days, they'd probably be joining in the family way soon, as well.

"You're looking all philosophical over there," Austin said from his place on one of the loveseats. Sierra leaned into him, her eyes sleepy. Leif was on the ground, playing with his little brother Colin, who wasn't all that little anymore.

"Just thinking about how much has changed in the past few years." He looked over at his family and smiled, though part of it was a bit sad. "I mean, just think about everything that's happened since Sierra walked into Montgomery Ink."

Sierra grinned, her eyes more alert. "Well, this big brute of a man pissed me off, but what can I say. He's just so lovable once you get to know him."

"That's our family motto," Maya put in from where she lay on the floor, her head on Jake's thigh. Border sat on the other side of Jake but had his hand in Maya's hair, slowly brushing the strands from her face. Their son, Noah, slept on Border's lap, his belly rising up and down with his tiny snores.

Austin kissed Sierra soundly on the mouth, and Leif made gagging sounds. Wes was pretty sure that any day now, that kid wouldn't think girls had cooties and would rather try kissing, but he didn't mention that.

"So, do we get the motto tattooed under the iris?" Miranda asked, a wide smile on her face. She sat next to Decker on their side of the couch with baby Micah on his dad's lap. Micah alternated between tugging on Decker's beard and crawling on the floor with their big dog that thought Micah was the best thing on plant Earth.

Of course, the dog wasn't the only animal in the room, as Wes and Jillian's new kitten, Sunny, was currently passed out on top of the dog's back, it's little belly up in the air and it's polydactyl paws spread.

Jillian had moved in with Wes as soon she was discharged from the hospital. They still had to deal with selling not only her house but also her father's, but they would get to it. They'd gotten the kitten soon after they started cohabitating because Jillian had mentioned one day that she wanted a pet and, of course, Wes couldn't deny her anything.

"How's your new tattoo feel?" Meghan asked from her spot on the couch between Miranda and Luc. "Actually, how do *all* of your new tattoos feel?" She smiled and leaned her head on her husband's shoulder. Their son, Cliff, lay on the floor near them, with their daughters Sasha and Emma playing with him. They'd already crawled over to play with Leif and the others earlier and would probably do so again. Wes liked the fact that all the cousins were being raised almost like siblings—much like some of his cousins and his siblings had.

"I like that you all chose different places to get them done," Luc said as he looked down at his own ink on his forearm. "Makes it special, you know?"

"I guess we're all Montgomerys, even though we aren't blood," Decker said with a wink, the statement heavy with meaning.

"Austin does great work," Jillian said as she patted her hip where her new Montgomery iris lay. She, Tabby, and Everly had gotten them together so they'd have them on their wedding days. He couldn't help but smile at the thought, and knew it was better than her having his name on her. Hell, he *knew* Maya and Austin wouldn't have allowed that. But the fact that the iris was also the logo for their work, family, and other parts of their lives, it was a little different than a name.

"So does Maya," Everly added quickly from her spot next to Storm.

"Yes, she does," Tabby said with a grin before leaning into Alex.

"Damn right I do," Maya said with a laugh.

"This does mean it's my turn next to do the ink," Austin added. "Though it seems to me we're out of wives and husbands to add to the mix unless we end up with another triad."

"I think one triad is good enough," Jake said as he kissed his husband's jaw and winked. "I don't think any of you could handle it."

They laughed before Leif looked up and smiled at Austin. "That means I'm next, right?"

Sierra let out a groan, and Austin shook his head. "You're still a ways away, kid," Austin growled, though his eyes smiled as he said it.

"Keep telling yourself that, Dad." Leif ducked as Austin playfully swiped at him and laughed.

"Oh!" Autumn exclaimed. "Did Griffin tell you the good news?" She winked at her husband, who just sighed. "Okay, I know he didn't but I can't hold it in any longer."

"What is it?" Marie asked as she leaned toward her son. "What's going on?"

"Well, they're going to finally announce it tomorrow, but I guess I can tell you guys if you promise to keep it off social media." Griffin glanced around the room, and everyone nodded. They understood what was meant to be kept secret and would never let it leak. "*Fatal Ties* is going to be made into a movie. It was not only optioned, but picked up. They'll start filming in two months."

Everyone screamed and shouted, and soon, Griffin had to push people off of him so he could breathe. Wes couldn't believe his little brother had come so far and was now going to have a damn *movie* with his name on it. How fucking cool was that?

"I'm so proud of you," their dad said as he cupped the back of Griffin's head. "And I'm really damn happy I'm going to be around to watch it."

Emotion clogged Wes's throat, and Jillian leaned into his side. While his father had beaten the cancer and was still going strong, Wes knew that Jillian was still healing over the loss of her dad. They talked about that and the shooting often, and even with a therapist to make sure they were always honest and open about their worries, it was still a heavy subject.

"You're a damn amazing writer, so here's to many more successes," Alex said, toasting his water glass to break the tension.

They toasted with him, and Wes watched as Alex laid his hand over Tabby's stomach when he thought no one else was looking. Well, that was interesting. Considering how much Alex had been through in the past, Wes was so freaking happy for the couple if what he thought was true.

Storm and Everly's twins woke up from where they'd been napping with Randy, their puppy, who wasn't a puppy any longer, and joined in to play with their cousins. Wes just grinned at the look on Storm's face. His own twin was one happy papa and still best friends with Wes's girl. Maybe if they were any other family, it might have been an issue, but they'd all gone through so much shit over the years, worrying about something that everyone said was in the past wasn't worth it.

"So, when do you think you'll be done with the warehouse?" Austin asked.

They'd had to close down work for two weeks due to the police investigation but thankfully they were well on their way to setting up each of the individual businesses within the main building.

They'd handed the lockbox over to the authorities when Jillian was still in the hospital, along with everything else they'd found. The current owners of the warehouse had been open and honest and truly had no idea about what had been going on before they bought the place. There were still criminal trials coming up for the men who had attacked Wes in the alley and then again in the warehouse, and even more charges for those who shot Jillian, broke into her home, and the other things they'd found on them. Wes wasn't sure exactly what would happen since he wasn't an attorney and all of it was out of his wheelhouse, but he'd do what he could to make sure that his family and homes were safe from whatever had tried to hurt them.

"A month if we stay on target," Wes said, clearing his thoughts from things he truly couldn't fix. Everly's bookstore had reopened with a special grand opening two weeks ago, and some of his crew was now working on other projects under the company umbrella. The Montgomerys were moving on and moving up—something he knew each and every member was a part of.

"That's good," his mother said with a shudder. "I'll be glad when my babies are able to work on other things." She was close enough to kiss Jillian's fully healed shoulder and give her soon-to-be daughter-in-law a hug.

Wes couldn't help but grin at the look on Jillian's face. His parents had pretty much adopted Jillian at this point, and he was sure that if he hadn't already been marrying her, they'd have found a way to make her a legal Montgomery anyway. It was just how they worked.

"There's another project coming up, though," Storm said with a wink, and Wes just grinned.

"Oh?" Miranda asked. "What is it?"

"Well, we can't tell you yet," Wes hedged. "But I can tell you that it might involve almost every

Montgomery here...and a few down in Colorado Springs."

Austin and Maya shared a knowing look, and Wes couldn't wait until they were ready to spill the details. That, however, would be for another time. Now, he just wanted to hold his woman and learn more about what had gone on with his family over the past few days since he hadn't really seen them.

"I'm happy," Jillian whispered as the others talked around them.

He leaned down and took her lips. "Yeah? Me, too."

"And I can't wait to be Mrs. Wesley Montgomery."

Wes narrowed his eyes. "What did I say about calling me Wesley?"

"That you love it and want that iced on our wedding cake?"

He growled and bit her lip before kissing away the sting. "You're going to give me gray hair, Jilli."

She studied his temple and frowned. "Going to?"

He growled again and whispered low, "You're going to pay for that."

"So you keep saying. But, Wes? I'll always be here to see what you have up your sleeve. Always."

And though his family still laughed and joked around him, he only had eyes for the woman in his arms. He hadn't been expecting her, and he knew she felt the same way about him. But in the end, he'd found his happily ever after—not in the person he'd thought he would find it with or even down the path that had seemed the easiest.

They'd fought and clawed for their happiness.

And that was the only way he knew how.

It was, after all, the Montgomery way.

Up Next?
The Montgomery Ink Series moves south to
Montgomery Ink: Colorado Springs and
FALLEN INK.

A Note from Carrie Ann

Thank you so much for reading **INKED MEMORIES**. I do hope if you liked this story, that you would please leave a review! Reviews help authors and readers.

I'm so honored that your read this book and love the Montgomerys as much as I do! Now don't be sad that Wes was the last Montgomery to get his book because there are MORE Montgomery Ink books on the way!

Not only will there be at least two more bonus novellas in the Montgomery Ink series, but the series continues with Fallen Ink (Montgomery Ink: Colorado Springs Book 1). Adrienne, Thea, and Roxie are Shep's sisters and ready for their HEAs. Adrienne is up first in FALLEN INK.

And don't forget Jake's brothers from INK ENDURING have their own series: The Gallagher Brothers series. LOVE RESTORED is Book 1. And Tabby's brothers from INK EXPOSED also have their own series, The Whiskey and Lies series. WHISKEY SECRETS is book 1.

Don't miss out on the Montgomery Ink World!

- Montgomery Ink (The Denver Montgomerys)
- Montgomery Ink: Colorado Springs (The Colorado Springs Montgomery Cousins)
- Gallagher Brothers (Jake's Brothers from Ink Enduring)
- Whiskey and Lies (Tabby's Brothers from Ink Exposed)

If you want to make sure you know what's coming next from me, you can sign up for my newsletter at www.CarrieAnnRyan.com; follow me on twitter at @CarrieAnnRyan, or like my Facebook page. I also have a Facebook Fan Club where we have trivia, chats, and other goodies. You guys are the reason I get to do what I do and I thank you.

Make sure you're signed up for my MAILING LIST so you can know when the next releases are available as well as find giveaways and FREE READS.

Happy Reading!

Montgomery Ink:
Book 0.5: Ink Inspired
Book 0.6: Ink Reunited
Book 1: Delicate Ink
Book 1.5: Forever Ink
Book 2: Tempting Boundaries
Book 3: Harder than Words
Book 4: Written in Ink
Book 4.5: Hidden Ink
Book 5: Ink Enduring
Book 6: Ink Exposed
Book 6.5: Adoring Ink
Book 6.6: Love, Honor, & Ink
Book 7: Inked Expressions
Book 7.5: Executive Ink
Book 8: Inked Memories

Montgomery Ink: Colorado Springs
Book 1: Fallen Ink (Coming Apr 2018)
Book 2: Restless Ink (Coming Aug 2018)

Want to keep up to date with the next Carrie Ann Ryan Release? Receive Text Alerts easily!
Text CARRIE to 24587

About Carrie Ann

Carrie Ann Ryan is the New York Times and USA Today bestselling author of contemporary and paranormal romance. Her works include the Montgomery Ink, Redwood Pack, Talon Pack, and Gallagher Brothers series, which have sold over 2.0 million books worldwide. She started writing while in graduate school for her advanced degree in chemistry and hasn't stopped since. Carrie Ann has written over fifty novels and novellas with more in the works. When she's not writing about bearded tattooed men or alpha wolves that need to find their mates, she's reading as much as she can and exploring the world of baking and gourmet cooking.

www.CarrieAnnRyan.com

More from Carrie Ann

Montgomery Ink:
Book 0.5: Ink Inspired
Book 0.6: Ink Reunited
Book 1: Delicate Ink
Book 1.5: Forever Ink
Book 2: Tempting Boundaries
Book 3: Harder than Words
Book 4: Written in Ink
Book 4.5: Hidden Ink
Book 5: Ink Enduring
Book 6: Ink Exposed
Book 6.5: Adoring Ink
Book 6.6: Love, Honor, & Ink
Book 7: Inked Expressions
Book 7.5: Executive Ink
Book 8: Inked Memories

Montgomery Ink: Colorado Springs
Book 1: Fallen Ink (Coming Apr 2018)
Book 2: Restless Ink (Coming Aug 2018)

The Gallagher Brothers Series:
A Montgomery Ink Spin Off Series
Book 1: Love Restored
Book 2: Passion Restored
Book 3: Hope Restored

The Whiskey and Lies Series:
A Montgomery Ink Spin Off Series
Book 1: Whiskey Secrets (Coming Jan 2018)
Book 2: Whiskey Reveals (Coming June 2018)

Book 3: Whiskey Undone (Coming Oct 2018)

The Talon Pack:
Book 1: Tattered Loyalties
Book 2: An Alpha's Choice
Book 3: Mated in Mist
Book 4: Wolf Betrayed
Book 5: Fractured Silence
Book 6: Destiny Disgraced
Book 7: Eternal Mourning (Coming Feb 2018)
Book 8: Strength Enduring (Coming July 2018)

Redwood Pack Series:
Prequel: An Alpha's Path
Book 1: A Taste for a Mate
Book 2: Trinity Bound
Book 2.5: A Night Away
Book 3: Enforcer's Redemption
Book 3.5: Blurred Expectations
Book 3.7: Forgiveness
Book 4: Shattered Emotions
Book 5: Hidden Destiny
Book 5.5: A Beta's Haven
Book 6: Fighting Fate
Book 6.5: Loving the Omega
Book 6.7: The Hunted Heart
Book 7: Wicked Wolf
The Complete Redwood Pack Box Set (Contains Books 1-7.7)

The Branded Pack Series:
(Written with Alexandra Ivy)
Book 1: Stolen and Forgiven
Book 2: Abandoned and Unseen
Book 3: Buried and Shadowed

Dante's Circle Series:
Book 1: Dust of My Wings
Book 2: Her Warriors' Three Wishes
Book 3: An Unlucky Moon
Book 3.5: His Choice
Book 4: Tangled Innocence
Book 5: Fierce Enchantment
Book 6: An Immortal's Song
Book 7: Prowled Darkness
The Complete Dante's Circle Series (Contains Books 1-7)

Holiday, Montana Series:
Book 1: Charmed Spirits
Book 2: Santa's Executive
Book 3: Finding Abigail
Book 4: Her Lucky Love
Book 5: Dreams of Ivory
The Complete Holiday, Montana Box Set (Contains Books 1-5)

Stand Alone Romances:
Finally Found You
Flame and Ink
Ink Ever After
Dropout

Delicate Ink

"If you don't turn that fucking music down, I'm going to ram this tattoo gun up a place no one on this earth should ever see."

Austin Montgomery lifted the needle from his client's arm so he could hold back a rough chuckle. He let his foot slide off the pedal so he could keep his composure. Dear Lord, his sister Maya clearly needed more coffee in her life.

Or for someone to turn down the fucking music in the shop.

"You're not even working, Maya. Let me have my tunes," Sloane, another artist, mumbled under his breath. Yeah, he didn't yell it. Didn't need to. No one wanted to yell at Austin's sister. The man might be as big as a house and made of pure muscle, but no one messed with Maya.

Not if they wanted to live.

"I'm sketching, you dumbass," Maya sniped, even though the smile in her eyes belied her wrath. His sister loved Sloane like a brother. Not that she didn't have enough brothers and sisters to begin with, but the Montgomerys always had their arms open for strays and spares.

Austin rolled his eyes at the pair's antics and stood up from his stool, his body aching from being bent over for too long. He refrained from saying that aloud as Maya and Sloane would have a joke for that. He usually preferred to have the other person in bed— or in the kitchen, office, doorway, etc—bent over, but that wasn't where he would allow his mind to go. As it was, he was too damn old to be sitting in that position for too long, but he wanted to get this sleeve done for his customer.

"Hold on a sec, Rick," he said to the man in the chair. "Want juice or anything? I'm going to stretch my legs and make sure Maya doesn't kill Sloane." He winked as he said it, just in case his client didn't get the joke.

People could be so touchy when siblings threatened each other with bodily harm even while they smiled as they said it.

"Juice sounds good," Rick slurred, a sappy smile on his face. "Don't let Maya kill you."

Rick blinked his eyes open, the adrenaline running through his system giving him the high that a few patrons got once they were in the chair for a couple hours. To Austin, there was nothing better than having Maya ink his skin—or doing it himself— and letting the needle do its work. He wasn't a pain junkie, far from it if he was honest with himself, but he liked the adrenaline that led the way into fucking fantastic art. While some people thought bodies were sacred and tattoos only marred them, he knew it differently. Art on canvas, any canvas, could have the potential to be art worth bleeding for. As such, he was particular as to who laid a needle on his skin. He only let Maya ink him when he couldn't do it himself. Maya was the same way. Whatever she couldn't do herself, he did.

They were brother and sister, friends, and co-owners of Montgomery Ink.

He and Maya had opened the shop a decade ago when she'd turned twenty. He probably could have opened it a few years earlier since he was eight years older than Maya, but he'd wanted to wait until she was ready. They were joint owners. It had never been his shop while she worked with him. They both had equal say, although with the way Maya spoke, sometimes her voice seemed louder. His deeper one carried just as much weight, even if he didn't yell as much.

Barely.

Sure, he wasn't as loud as Maya, but he got his point across when needed. His voice held control and authority.

He picked up a juice box for Rick from their mini-fridge and turned down the music on his way back. Sloane scowled at him, but the corner of his mouth twitched as if he held back a laugh.

"Thank God one of you has a brain in his head," Maya mumbled in the now quieter room. She rolled her eyes as both he and Sloane flipped her off then went back to her sketch. Yeah, she could have gotten up to turn the music down herself, but then she couldn't have vented her excess energy at the two of them. That was just how his sister worked, and there would be no changing that.

He went back to his station situated in the back so he had the corner space, handed Rick his juice, then rubbed his back. Damn, he was getting old. Thirty-eight wasn't that far up there on the scales, but ever since he'd gotten back from New Orleans, he hadn't been able to shake the weight of something off of his chest.

He needed to be honest. He'd started feeling this way since before New Orleans. He'd gone down to the city to visit his cousin Shep and try to get out of his funk. He'd broken up with Shannon right before then; however, in reality, it wasn't as much a breakup as a lack of connection and communication. They hadn't cared about each other enough to move on to the next level, and as sad as that was, he was fine with it. If he couldn't get up the energy to pursue a woman beyond a couple of weeks or months of heat, then he knew he was the problem. He just didn't know the solution. Shannon hadn't been the first woman who had ended the relationship in that fashion. There'd been Brenda, Sandrine, and another one named Maggie.

He'd cared for all of them at the time. He wasn't a complete asshole, but he'd known deep down that they weren't going to be with him forever, and they thought the same of him. He also knew that it was time to actually find a woman to settle down with. If he wanted a future, a family, he was running out of time.

Going to New Orleans hadn't worked out in the least considering, at the time, Shep was falling in love with a pretty blonde named Shea. Not that Austin begrudged the man that. Shep had been his best friend growing up, closer to him than his four brothers and three sisters. It'd helped that he and Shep were the same age while the next of his siblings, the twins Storm and Wes, were four years younger.

His parents had taken their time to have eight kids, meaning he was a full fifteen years older than the baby, Miranda, but he hadn't cared. The eight of them, most of his cousins, and a few strays were as close as ever. He'd helped raise the youngest ones as an older brother but had never felt like he had to. His parents, Marie and Harry, loved each of their kids equally and had put their whole beings into their roles as parents. Every single concert, game, ceremony, or even parent-teacher meeting was attended by at least one of them. On the good days, the ones where Dad could get off work and Mom had the day off from Montgomery Inc., they both would attend. They loved their kids.

He loved being a Montgomery.

The sound of Sloane's needle buzzing as he sang whatever tune played in his head made Austin grin.

And he fucking *loved* his shop.

Every bare brick and block of polished wood, every splash of black and hot pink—colors he and Maya had fought on and he'd eventually given in to—made him feel at home. He'd taken the family crest and symbol, the large MI surrounded by a broken floral circle, and used it as their logo. His brothers, Storm and Wes, owned Montgomery Inc., a family construction company that their father had once owned and where their mother had worked at his side before they'd retired. They, too, used the same logo since it meant family to them.

In fact, the MI was tattooed on every single immediate family member—including his parents. His own was on his right forearm tangled in the rest of his sleeve but given a place of meaning. It meant Montgomery Iris—*open your eyes, see the beauty, remember who you are.* It was only natural to use it for their two respective companies.

Not that the Ink vs Inc. wasn't confusing as hell, but fuck, they were Montgomerys. They could do whatever they wanted. As long as they were together, they'd get through it.

Montgomery Ink was just as much his home as his house on the ravine. While Shep had gone on to work at Midnight Ink and created another family there, Austin had always wanted to own his shop. Maya growing up to want to do the same thing had only helped.

Montgomery Ink was now a thriving business in downtown Denver right off 16th Street Mall. They were near parking, food, and coffee. There really wasn't more he needed. The drive in most mornings could suck once he got on I-25, but it was worth it to live out in Arvada. The 'burbs around Denver made it easy to live in one area of the city and work in another. Commutes, though hellish at rush hour, weren't as bad as some. This way he got the city living when it came to work and play, and the option to hide behind the trees pressed up against the foothills of the Rocky Mountains once he got home.

It was the best of both worlds.

At least for him.

Austin got back on his stool and concentrated on Rick's sleeve for another hour before calling it quits. He needed a break for his lower back, and Rick needed a break from the pain. Not that Rick was feeling much since the man currently looked like he'd just gotten laid—pain freaks, Austin loved them—but he didn't want to push either of them too far. Also, Plus Rick's arm had started to swell slightly from all the shading and multiple colors. They'd do another session, the last, hopefully, in a month or so when both of them could work it in their schedules and then finish up.

Austin scowled at the computer at the front of shop, his fingers too big for the damn keys on the prissy computer Maya had demanded they buy.

"Fuck!"

He'd just deleted Rick's whole account because he couldn't find the right button.

"Maya, get your ass over here and fix this. I don't know what the hell I did."

Maya lifted one pierced brow as she worked on a lower back tattoo for some teenage girl who didn't look old enough to get ink in the first place.

"I'm busy, Austin. You're not an idiot, though evidence at the moment points to the contrary. Fix it yourself. I can't help it if you have ape hands."

Austin flipped her off then took a sip of his Coke, wishing he had something stronger considering he hated paperwork. "I was fine with the old keyboard and the PC, Maya. You're the one who wanted to go with the Mac because it looked pretty."

"Fuck you, Austin. I wanted a Mac because I like the software."

Austin snorted while trying to figure out how to find Rick's file. He was pretty sure it was a lost cause at this point. "You hate the software as much as I do. You hit the damn red X and close out files more than I do. Everything's in the wrong place, and the keyboard is way too fucking dainty."

"I'm going to go with Austin on this one," Sloane added in, his beefy hands in the air.

"See? I'm not alone."

Maya let out a breath. "We can get another keyboard for you and Gigantor's hands, but we need to keep the Mac."

"And why is that?" he demanded.

"Because we just spent a whole lot of money on it, and once it goes, we can get another PC. Fuck the idea that everything can be all in one. I can't figure it out either." She held up a hand. "And don't even think about breaking it. I'll know, Austin. I *always* know."

Austin held back a grin. He wouldn't be surprised if the computer met with an earlier than expected unfortunate fate now that Maya had relented.

Right then, however, that idea didn't help. He needed to find Rick's file.

"Callie!" Austin yelled over the buzz of needles and soft music Maya had allowed them to play.

"What?" His apprentice came out of the break room, a sketchbook in one hand and a smirk on her face. She'd dyed her hair again so it had black and red highlights. It looked good on her, but honestly, he never knew what color she'd have next. "Break something on the computer again with those big man hands?"

"Shut up, minion," he teased. Callie was an up-and-coming artist, and if she kept on the track she was on, he and Maya knew she'd be getting her own chair at Montgomery Ink soon. Not that he'd tell Callie that, though. He liked keeping her on her toes. She reminded him of his little sister Miranda so much that he couldn't help but treat her as such.

She pushed him out of the way and groaned. "Did you have to press *every* button as you rampaged through the operating system?"

Austin could have sworn he felt his cheeks heat, but since he had a thick enough beard, he knew no one would have been able to tell.

Hopefully.

He hated feeling as if he didn't know what he was doing. It wasn't as if he didn't know how to use a computer. He wasn't an idiot. He just didn't know *this* computer. And it bugged the shit out of him.

After a couple of keystrokes and a click of the mouse, Callie stepped back with a smug smile on her face. "Okay, boss, you're all ready to go, and Rick's file is back where it should be. What else do you need from me?"

He bopped her on the head, messing up her red and black hair he knew she spent an hour on every morning with a flat iron. He couldn't help it.

"Go clean a toilet or something."

Callie rolled her eyes. "I'm going to go sketch. And you're welcome."

"Thanks for fixing the damn thing. And really, go clean the bathroom."

"Not gonna do it," she sang as she skipped to the break room.

"You really have no control over your apprentice," Sloane commented from his station.

Because he didn't want that type of control with her. Well, hell, his mind kept going to that dark place every few minutes it seemed.

"Shut up, asshole."

"I see your vocabulary hasn't changed much," Shannon purred from the doorway.

He closed his eyes and prayed for patience. Okay, maybe he'd lied to himself when he said it was mutual and easy to break up with her. The damn woman kept showing up. He didn't think she wanted him, but she didn't want him to forget her either.

He did not understand women.

Especially this one.

"What do you want, Shannon?" he bit out, needing that drink now more than ever.

She sauntered over to him and scraped her long, red nail down his chest. He'd liked that once. Now, not even a little. They were decent together when they'd dated, but he'd had to hide most of himself from her. She'd never tasted the edge of his flogger or felt his hand on her ass when she'd been bent over his lap. That hadn't been what she wanted, and Austin was into the kind of kink that meant he wanted what he wanted when he wanted. It didn't mean he wanted it every time.

Not that Shannon would ever understand that.

"Oh, baby, you know what I want."

He barely resisted the urge to roll his eyes. As he took a step back, he saw the gleam in her eyes and decided to head it off at the pass. He was in no mood to play her games, or whatever she wanted to do that night. He wanted to go home, drink a beer, and forget this oddly annoying day.

"If you don't want ink, then I don't know what you're doing here, Shannon. We're done." He tried to say it quietly, but his voice was deep, and it carried.

"How could you be so cruel?" She pouted.

"Oh, for the love of God," Maya sneered. "Go home, little girl. You and Austin are through, and I'm pretty sure it was mutual. Oh, and you're not getting any ink here. You're not getting Austin's hands on you this way, and there's no way in hell I'm putting my art on you. Not if you keep coming back to bug the man you didn't really date in the first place."

"Bi—" Shannon cut herself off as Austin glared. Nobody called his sister a bitch. Nobody.

"Goodbye, Shannon." Jesus, he was too old for this shit.

"Fine. I see how it is. Whatever. You were only an okay lay anyway." She shook her ass as she left, bumping into a woman in a linen skirt and blouse.

The woman, whose long honey-brown hair hung in waves down to her breasts, raised a brow. "I see your business has an...interesting clientele."

Austin clenched his jaw. Seriously the wrong thing to say after Shannon.

"If you've got a problem, you can head on right back to where you came from, Legs," he bit out, his voice harsher than he'd intended.

She stiffened then raised her chin, a clear sense of disdain radiating off of her.

Oh yes, he knew who this was, legs and all. Ms. Elder. He hadn't caught a first name. Hadn't wanted to. She had to be in her late twenties, maybe, and owned the soon-to-be-opened boutique across the street. He'd seen her strut around in her too-tall heels and short skirts but hadn't been formally introduced.

Not that he wanted an introduction.

She was too damn stuffy and ritzy for his taste. Not only her store but the woman herself. The look of disdain on her face made him want to show her the door and never let her back in.

He knew what he looked like. Longish dark brown hair, thick beard, muscles covered in ink with a hint of more ink coming out of his shirt. He looked like a felon to some people who didn't know the difference, though he'd never seen the inside of a jail cell in his life. But he knew people like Ms. Elder. They judged people like him. And that one eyebrow pissed him the fuck off.

He didn't want this woman's boutique across the street from him. He'd liked it when it was an old record store. People didn't glare at his store that way. Now he had to walk past the mannequins with the rich clothes and tiny lacy scraps of things if he wanted a fucking coffee from the shop next door.

Damn it, this woman pissed him off, and he had no idea why.

"Nice to meet you too. Callie!" he shouted, his eyes still on Ms. Elder as if he couldn't pull his gaze from her. Her green eyes never left his either, and the uncomfortable feeling in his gut wouldn't go away.

Callie ran up beside him and held out her hand. "Hi, I'm Callie. How can I help you?"

Ms. Elder blinked once. Twice. "I think I made a mistake," she whispered.

Fuck. Now he felt like a heel. He didn't know what it was with this woman, but he couldn't help but act like an ass. She hadn't even done anything but lift an eyebrow at him, and he'd already set out to hate her.

Callie shook her head then reached for Ms. Elder's elbow. "I'm sure you haven't. Ignore the growly, bearded man over there. He needs more caffeine. And his ex was just in here; that alone would make anyone want to jump off the Royal Gorge. So, tell me, how can I help you? Oh! And what's your name?"

Ms. Elder followed Callie to the sitting area with leather couches and portfolios spread over the coffee table and then sat down.

"I'm Sierra, and I want a tattoo." She looked over her shoulder and glared at Austin. "Or, at least, I thought I did."

Austin held back a wince when she turned her attention from him and cursed himself. Well, fuck. He needed to learn not to put his foot in his mouth, but damn it, how was he supposed to know she wanted a tattoo? For all he knew, she wanted to come in there and look down on the place. That was his own prejudice coming into play. He needed to make it up to her. After all, they were neighbors now. However, from the cross look on her face and the feeling in the room, he knew that he wasn't going to be able to make it up to her today. He'd let Callie help her out to start with, and then he'd make sure he was the one who laid ink on her skin.

After all, it was the least he could do. Besides, his hands all of a sudden—or not so suddenly if he really thought about it—wanted to touch that delicate skin of hers and find out her secrets.

Austin cursed. He wouldn't let his thoughts go down that path. She'd break under his care, under his needs. Sure, Sierra Elder might be hot, but she wasn't the woman for him.

If he knew anything, he knew *that* for sure.

Love Restored

In the first of a Montgomery Ink spin-off series from NYT Bestselling Author Carrie Ann Ryan, a broken man uncovers the truth of what it means to take a second chance with the most unexpected woman...

Graham Gallagher has seen it all. And when tragedy struck, lost it all. He's been the backbone of his brothers, the one they all rely on in their lives and business. And when it comes to falling in love and creating a life, he knows what it's like to have it all and watch it crumble. He's done with looking for another person to warm his bed, but apparently he didn't learn his lesson because the new piercer at Montgomery Ink tempts him like no other.

Blake Brennen may have been born a trust fund baby, but she's created a whole new life for herself in the world of ink, piercings, and freedom. Only the ties she'd thought she'd cut long ago aren't as severed as she'd believed. When she finds Graham constantly in her path, she knows from first glance that he's the wrong kind of guy for her. Except that Blake excels at making the wrong choice and Graham might be the ultimate temptation for the bad girl she'd thought long buried.

Tattered Loyalties

When the great war between the Redwoods and the Centrals occurred three decades ago, the Talon Pack risked their lives for the side of good. After tragedy struck, Gideon Brentwood became the Alpha of the Talons. But the Pack's stability is threatened, and he's forced to take mate—only the one fate puts in his path is the woman he shouldn't want.

Though the daughter of the Redwood Pack's Beta, Brie Jamenson has known peace for most of her life. When she finds the man who could be her mate, she's shocked to discover Gideon is the Alpha wolf of the Talon Pack. As a submissive, her strength lies in her heart, not her claws. But if her new Pack disagrees or disapproves, the consequences could be fatal.

As the worlds Brie and Gideon have always known begin to shift, they must face their challenges together in order to help their Pack and seal their bond. But when the Pack is threatened from the inside, Gideon doesn't know who he can trust and Brie's life could be forfeit in the crossfire. It will take the strength of an Alpha and the courage of his mate to realize where true loyalties lie.

CPSIA information can be obtained
at www.ICGtesting.com
Printed in the USA
LVOW07s1657171017
552750LV00012B/1293/P